PUF

GRIZZLY TALES

The characters in these stories are some of the most horrible, rudest, most revolting and gruesome to ever exist, but they all get their just desserts in the most grizzly, scary and fitting way possible! Timothy is a hideous child who refuses to eat his mother's food and his demise at the hands of the Spaghetti Man is particularly unpleasant. And Tania and Peregrine are mysteriously cured of their foul mouths when they visit the barber, and return with slightly shorter tongues! But the new nanny for Tristram and Candy is of the very grizzly kind indeed and has just about had enough of these two wicked children.

Jamie Rix cleverly combines the humorous with the fantastic and unexpected in these highly amusing cautionary tales that will appeal to all children, not just the gruesome!

Jamie Rix is a television producer of comedy and a comedy writer for such programmes as *Not the Nine O'Clock News*, *Smith and Jones* and *Comic Relief*. *Grizzly Tales for Gruesome Kids* is Jamie's first book and was shortlisted in the 9–11 category of the 1990 Smarties Prize and declared overall winner by the panel of children's judges. Jamie Rix lives in south London with his wife and two sons, Ben and Jack, to whom this book is dedicated.

GRIZZLY TALES
FOR
GRUESOME KIDS

Stories by
JAMIE RIX

Illustrated by BOBBIE SPARGO

PUFFIN BOOKS

PUFFIN BOOKS

Published by the Penguin Group
Penguin Books Ltd, 27 Wrights Lane, London W8 5TZ, England
Penguin Books USA Inc., 375 Hudson Street, New York, New York 10014, USA
Penguin Books Australia Ltd, Ringwood, Victoria, Australia
Penguin Books Canada Ltd, 10 Alcorn Avenue, Toronto, Ontario, Canada M4V 3B2
Penguin Books (NZ) Ltd, 182–190 Wairau Road, Auckland 10, New Zealand

Penguin Books Ltd, Registered Offices: Harmondsworth, Middlesex, England

First published by André Deutsch Limited 1990
Published in Puffin Books 1992
1 3 5 7 9 10 8 6 4 2

Printed in England by Clays Ltd, St Ives plc

To Ben and Jack
who were scared first.

Contents

The New Nanny

There is a family, living in South London, that has the collective intelligence of a dead ant. Mr Frightfully-Busy spends all his time at the office and wears nasty pink ties to work. Mrs Frightfully-Busy helps out in a gift shop in the King's Road. She flits around the shelves all day doing absolutely nothing, trying to avoid serving any customers. Their children are called Tristram and Candy. They hardly know their parents, because their parents are never at home, and they spend most of their days being completely unpleasant to their long suffering nanny.

Mrs Mac is sixty-three years old and was Mrs Frightfully-Busy's nanny when Mrs Frightfully-Busy was a child. Now Mrs Mac has to look after Tristram and Candy, which is no easy task.

In the morning when Mrs Mac dresses the children, they lay traps for her by hanging their duvets over the door. Once she is entangled in their quilts, the children leap off the top bunk, tie her up with string and threat-

en to push her out of the window. When she cooks their
lunch they put the bits they don't want onto her chair, so
that when Mrs Mac sits down she gets fish fingers all over
her bottom. At bath time they pretend to be asleep in the
water. When she leans forward to wake them, they spit
water in her face. When it is time for bed, they call her
names, hide in the airing cupboard, switch on the telly,
refuse to brush their teeth, pretend they are ill, find an
interesting book that they want her to read, and run to
their mummy and daddy to tell lies about how badly Mrs
Mac looks after them. The worst thing is that their parents
always believe their lies, because in their eyes Tristram and
Candy can do no wrong.

One day Tristram and Candy went too far.

"Mrs Mac beat us, today," they lied to their parents.

Mrs Frightfully-Busy looked up from her Martini. "She
beat my precious little angels?"

"Yes," said Candy, "so hard that I cried."

"That's not on," said Mr Frightfully-Busy. "Remind me
to tell Mrs Mac never to do it again."

"I should think so too," added Mrs Frightfully-Busy.
"Now run along children, Mummy and Daddy want a
little peace and quiet."

"She beat us with your golf clubs, Daddy."

"My golf clubs!" Mr Frightfully-Busy was out of his
chair in a flash. "Did she break them?"

"Oh yes," whimpered Tristram, who was a very good
actor, "across the back of my legs!"

"Those golf clubs cost me a fortune!" he shouted as
he stormed out of the room. Then they heard him bellow
from the foot of the stairs, "Mrs Mac. You're fired. Pack

your bags and get out of this house at once!"

Poor old Mrs Mac. She had worked for the family for forty years and now she was being thrown out, because of one malicious, spiteful, childish lie.

The next day Mrs Frightfully-Busy was in a panic. There was nobody to look after her children and *she* certainly wasn't going to do it. She looked in the telephone directory under Nanny. All the agencies seemed to be exactly the same. All except one. ANIMAL MAGIC, it read. WE PROVIDE NANNIES TO SUIT *ALL* CHILDREN. NO CHILD TOO DIFFICULT TO HANDLE.

Mrs Frightfully-Busy phoned them up.

"They are the most adorable little children you could ever wish to meet," she said to the voice at the other end of the phone. "Dear, sweet Tristram is so kind and gentle, and Candy is really no trouble at all. I hardly know she's there sometimes."

"There'll be somebody round in half an hour," said the voice and Mrs Frightfully-Busy heaved an enormous sigh of relief.

Half an hour later there was a ring at the door.

"Come and meet your new nanny," Mrs Frightfully-Busy shouted to Tristram and Candy, as she opened the front door. There was nobody there.

"Down here!" hissed a voice on the front path.

Mrs Frightfully-Busy looked down.

"Animal Magic Nannies at your service," added the thirty-five foot python as it slithered across the doormat and into the hall.

Tristram and Candy stopped dead at the foot of the stairs. Their jaws dropped open in disbelief. A long brown snake

3

wearing a starched white apron, and carrying a handbag, had just slid into their house. Their mother must have gone stark staring bonkers and, to cap it all, she hadn't even noticed.

"I'll be back at six! Have a good day," said Mrs Frightfully-Busy, picking her car keys up from the hall table and sweeping out of the front door. The door slammed shut and Tristram and Candy were left alone with their new nanny.

"What would you like to do today, children?" said the python. Its red tongue darted in and out of its mouth. The children were too frightened to answer.

"Shall we play a game of snakes and ladders?"

Candy couldn't help herself. She screamed. "Don't eat us."

"Eat you," said the snake. "Don't be silly. I'm here to look after you. Just treat me as you would any other nanny."

That was what Tristram and Candy needed to hear. From that moment on they reverted to their normal, horrible selves.

At lunch they stuck their nanny's tail in a pan of boiling water. In the park they scattered tin tacks on the path, which pierced her skin as she slithered over them. They wrapped her up in their parents' bath towels and stuck her head down the lavatory. They knotted her around the legs of their bunk beds and left her tied up all afternoon, while they watched the telly. They even staked her out in the back garden and waited for the birds to come down and peck at her, thinking she was an enormous worm.

By the time Mr and Mrs Frightfully-Busy came back

that night, the new nanny was a nervous wreck. She was more scared of the children than they were of her. No sooner did she hear the front door open, than she was out of that house faster than a speeding bullet.

"How was the new nanny?" said Mr Frightfully-Busy.

"Really cruel," lied the children.

"Do you know," said Tristram, "she nearly strangled me when she gave me a hug."

"Then she's never coming back into this house!" declared Mrs Frightfully-Busy.

The next morning Mrs Frightfully-Busy phoned ANI-MAL MAGIC again. "The nanny you sent yesterday was completely useless!" she said.

"Yes," said the voice at the other end, "I know. She's told us all about your children. We'll send you a more suitable nanny today. She'll drop in in about fifteen minutes."

Sure enough, fifteen minutes later the doorbell rang. Mrs Frightfully-Busy picked up her car keys and opened the door.

"'Bye children. The new nanny's here. See you later." She didn't even stop to find out who the new nanny was.

Tristram and Candy rushed to the open door to see for themselves, but they could see no one.

"Cooee," said a voice above them. But before they could look up an enormous, hairy black spider dropped down from the roof of the porch.

"I'm the new nanny," said the spider as she bit through her web and scuttled into the hall. "You must be Tristram and Candy. I've heard so much about you."

Tristram and Candy had turned white.

"I h . . . h . . . h . . . hate spiders," stammered Tristram.

"Me too," agreed Candy.

"Don't be silly," said the spider. "I wouldn't harm a fly." She paused for a moment to think. "Well, maybe a fly, but I wouldn't harm you."

"Oh good," said Candy, who was already thinking up some awful prank to play on the spider.

"Now where shall we begin?" said the nanny.

"In the bathroom," fibbed Candy. "We always have a bath after breakfast."

So up to the bathroom they went.

It is a well known fact that spiders hate water. The children's nanny was no exception. Her own father had nearly drowned once in a hand basin. Tristram and Candy deliberately kept splashing her.

"Stop it," she screamed.

The children gained the upper hand.

6

"Shan't!" shouted Tristram, filling a bucket full of water and pouring it over his nanny's head. She retreated into a corner and curled up into a furry ball. The children jumped out of the water, picked her up, threw her into the bath and pulled the plug out. The spider was caught in a raging whirlpool that sucked her down towards the drain.

Tristram and Candy poked her with a flannel and laughed.

The spider suddenly sprang open, her legs flailing about in the torrent, and with one mighty effort she clawed her way to the edge of the bath and climbed out. Tristram offered her his towel.

"What can we do now?" he smirked.

"I know," said Candy to the spider. "You can build

us a climbing frame in the garden."

The new nanny was wet and miserable as she set about spinning the children a climbing frame. Every time she stopped to catch her breath, they shouted, "More! It's still not big enough!" until, finally, her web stretched from one garden fence to the other. At its highest point it reached the chimney pot on top of the roof, and it fell away steeply across the entire length of the garden to Mr Frightfully-Busy's compost heap. It looked like a circus safety-net – the sort trapeze artists use in the big top.

The spider collapsed at the end of her ordeal and fell asleep from exhaustion.

"A fine nanny she's turned out to be," said Tristram. "Let's teach her a lesson she'll never forget."

So they pulled down the climbing frame, and while she slept they wrapped her up in her own web.

That was how Mr and Mrs Frightfully-Busy found her. Cold and damp. The children's unlucky prisoner.

"This looks like a fun game," said Mr Frightfully-Busy. "What's it called?"

"Poke the nanny," said Candy prodding the spider with a sharp stick.

"What a super idea," said Mrs Frightfully-Busy. Then, "Thank you, nanny, you can go now. We'll see you in the morning."

Mr Frightfully-Busy picked up the spider, put her in a wheelbarrow and dumped her on the pavement.

In bed that night, Tristram was asked what he thought of his new nanny. "Even crueller than the snake," he lied. "Do you know what she did? She tied her web around our ankles and hung us upside down from the ceiling all morning."

8

"We don't like her," chipped in Candy.

"Then she's never coming back into this house!" declared Mrs Frightfully-Busy.

The following morning she rang up the ANIMAL MAGIC NANNY AGENCY for the third time. "I'll give you one last chance to send me a nanny who can look after my children properly!" she shouted down the phone.

"Yes, Mrs Frightfully-Busy. As it happens, we have the perfect nanny right here in the office. I'll send her over straight away," said the voice at the other end.

On this particular morning, Mrs Frightfully-Busy couldn't even wait for the new nanny to arrive. She just had to get off to work.

"I'll leave the door on the latch," she said to the children. "When the new nanny arrives, just tell her to come straight in." Then she pulled the door to and left Tristram and Candy alone in the house.

Seconds later they heard squelchy footsteps outside the front door.

"Come straight in!" shouted Tristram, who was standing on a chair waiting to bonk his new nanny on the head with a baseball bat as she came through the door.

The door swung open and the squelchy footsteps came in.

CLONK! Tristram brought the bat down hard on the nanny's head. Candy squealed with delight. It was such a clever trick.

Then they both stopped laughing. The new nanny blinked and continued walking. She stopped in the middle of the hall. Water dripped off her scaly back and formed tiny puddles on the carpet. She flicked her tail.

"I'm your new nanny," said the alligator. "Any nonsense,

and I'll eat you for breakfast."

"We're not scared of you, are we?" said Candy, cockily.

"No way," said Tristram. "You're just the nanny. Take that!" and he hit the alligator on the head again.

It was all over in a flash. Two snaps, two gulps and the children were gone.

When Mr and Mrs Frightfully-Busy came home that night they couldn't find the children anywhere. Mrs Frightfully-Busy did, however, find a very sleepy alligator curled up in the airing cupboard. "Are you the nanny?" she said.

"Yes," said the alligator, opening one eye.

"Where are the children?" said Mr Frightfully-Busy, hiding behind his wife.

"I've eaten them," said the alligator, licking her lips.

"Although I must say they tasted horrible, but then little liars always do."

"Get out of this house immediately!" shouted Mr Frightfully-Busy.

"That won't be necessary," replied the alligator, raising her head and flashing a fearsome set of teeth. She edged forward and Mr and Mrs Frightfully-Busy backed away down the stairs. Then the alligator stood up on her back legs and just as they thought she was going to pounce, she laid two large, white eggs.

"Excuse me," said the alligator, brushing past Mr and Mrs Frightfully-Busy. "Places to go. People to see." And she left.

Mr Frightfully-Busy sat his wife down, then went over to the eggs to take a closer look. They each had a long crack down one side. As Mr Frightfully-Busy watched, the cracks grew bigger.

"The eggs are hatching!" he said to his wife. "We're about to be invaded by baby alligators!"

There was a crunch, then a snap. Something scraped against the edge of the shell. Then the first finger emerged, followed by an arm, a neck, then a head. It was Tristram.

"My baby!" shouted Mrs Frightfully-Busy rushing over and wrapping her arms round him.

Candy suddenly burst through the shell of the second egg.

"My two babies!" she wailed. "What happened?"

"We were rude and nasty to the nanny," said Tristram.

"And she ate us," added Candy.

It was the first time they had ever told the plain truth.

There was a ring at the front door. Mr Frightfully-Busy

left his family to answer it. It was Mrs Mac.

"I was wondering if you'd found a new nanny yet for Tristram and Candy," she said.

"No," said Mr Frightfully-Busy.

"In that case, would you like me to come back?" said Mrs Mac.

Mr Frightfully-Busy didn't know what to say. Then he remembered the snake, the spider and that awful alligator. "Yes please," he said, without hesitation. "When can you start?"

"Right away," said Mrs Mac, "if you'll help me in with my things."

"Certainly," said Mr Frightfully-Busy, and he bent down to pick up her suitcases. One was made of snake skin. One was all black and hairy (and looked remarkably like a spider) and the third, the biggest of them all, was made from the skin of an alligator.

The One-Tailed, Two-Footed, Three-Bellied, Four-Headed, Five-Fingered, Six-Chinned, Seven-Winged, Eight-Eyed, Nine-Nosed, Ten-Toothed Monster

There is a village in India called Jaisalmer, which is famous throughout the world for the standard of its education. Its children are simply the best mathematicians in the world. If you listen very closely, I'll tell you why.

Four hundred years ago, Jaisalmer was like a ghost town. The streets were always empty. Front doors were always shut, windows locked. There were no birds or animals or flowers. The people were sad. The children never laughed. The village was paralysed by fear.

In the caves, just outside the village, there lived a hideous monster; one-tailed, two-footed, three-bellied, four-headed, five-fingered, six-chinned, seven-winged, eight-eyed, nine-nosed and ten toothed. At night, so legend told, it went in search of food. It slipped, like a shadow, through the village, smashing houses, killing animals and gobbling anyone who tried to stop it.

In the daytime while the monster slept, the people would rebuild their village. But come night fall, when

13

they heard that terrible roar, which sounded for all the world like "I'm coming to eat you!", they would drop their tools and rush for safety.

The village elders had offered a reward of one thousand rupees to anyone who could kill this monster and rid the village of its terrible curse. Many brave men had tried. They had ridden off into the desert, armed with spears and knives, promising great things, but none had ever returned.

There was a boy called Tulsidor who went to the local school. He was tall for his age and very strong. His father was a farmer, and after school Tulsidor would help him to load up the bullock cart with vegetables for market. Sometimes his schoolmates would tease him because of his size, but Tulsidor would never take offence. He just laughed along with the rest of them, and everybody liked him.

There was one thing, however, that was guaranteed to wipe the smile off Tulsidor's face. Mathematics. He had never been any good at sums, even though his mother gave him extra tuition after school. In class, the teacher would write some numbers on the blackboard.

"Right," she'd say, "What is three plus three?" Then she'd look around the room for someone to answer. Tulsidor would always pretend to be writing something down when she looked at him.

"Tulsidor. Perhaps you could tell us what three plus three is?"

"Twenty?" he'd guess. "Thirty? A hundred? I don't know. Is it more or less?"

"A little less," the teacher would reply. "What are we

going to do with you?"

Tulsidor's class had an important maths exam the following week, and it didn't take a donkey to work out that Tulsidor was going to fail.

That night Tulsidor was sitting out on the verandah studying his sums. "What's one plus two, Mum?" he shouted.

"Three," replied his mother from the kitchen.

"And two plus one?"

"Still three," said his mother.

His father came in from working in the fields. "Better get in now, Tulsidor," he said. "It's nearly night fall. The monster will be out looking for his supper shortly."

Tulsidor nodded vaguely, but he hadn't heard a word. He was still trying to work out how two plus one and one plus two could possibly have the same answer.

He got up and wandered over to the cow shed where his father had locked the bullocks up for the night. Tulsidor opened the stable door and leaned in. "Now, Dad's got three bullocks," he said to himself. "One, two, three." He counted them several times and wrote it down in his exercise book. "So if I put one of them into a separate stall, how many have I got left?"

There was a terrible roar behind him. The earth quivered, the shed shook and the bullocks crashed into the stalls with fright. Tulsidor could hear his mother's faraway voice calling him.

"Tulsidor! Tulsidor! Where are you?"

He had been so wrapped up in his work that he hadn't noticed the sun going down. Night had fallen. The monster was out of its cave.

Then he heard the roar again, only this time it was closer. "I'm coming to eat you!"

An ice-cold wind rushed through his hair, snatched the exercise book from his hand and knocked him to the ground. Eight fiery eyes stared at him from out of the darkness. Two enormous feet crashed through the surrounding trees, and Tulsidor fainted as four scaly heads popped up over the top of the cow shed.

When he woke up, Tulsidor was in the monster's cave. He couldn't see very well, because it was so dark, but over in the corner he could just make out the shape of the monster, sitting on its haunches, reading something. Tulsidor moved very slowly. If he could just reach the entrance to the cave he was sure he could escape. After all he was the fastest runner in his class.

He stood up and edged forward, holding onto the rocks for support. He felt something roll away from under his hand. Something cold and hard. Before he could stop himself, he had screamed. It was a pile of bones. The monster turned round to see what the noise was and Tulsidor froze with fear. It was every bit as ugly as he'd been told.

One tail, two feet, three bellies, four heads, five fingers, six chins, seven wings, eight eyes, nine noses and ten teeth!

"Hullo," said the monster, "having problems with your maths?"

"What?" said Tulsidor, who couldn't believe what he had just heard.

"Problems with your sums?" said the Monster as it flew a little nearer.

"Well, as it happens, yes," said Tulsidor. He was gob-smacked.

"Do you want a hand with them?" said the monster.

"Aren't you going to eat me?" asked Tulsidor.

"Eat you? Yuck." The monster screwed up its four faces into a look of disgust. "I'm a vegetarian."

"But you eat people."

"Not me," said the monster. "I go into the village to make friends, but nobody wants to know me. I will admit that some of the animals run off when they see me coming, but I can't help looking the way I do. And I have flattened a few houses, but my feet are so big and clumsy. It's very hard to walk on tiptoe, you know."

There was a moment's silence, then Tulsidor said, "What's one and two?"

"Easy," said the monster. "Three. Now I'll ask you one. How many wings have I got?"

Tulsidor counted them. "Seven," he said.

"And how many bellies?"

"Three!" shouted Tulsidor, who was starting to enjoy himself.

"Which makes?"

Tulsidor looked puzzled.

"Count my teeth," said the monster, grinning cheesily.

"Ten."

"Correct," said the monster. "That's the first sum you've ever got right."

Tulsidor spent three days and three nights in the monster's cave. When he came out he had learnt the answer to every sum possible by counting up bits of the monster's body.

He came top in his maths exam, and his teacher was astonished.

"Who taught you to count, Tulsidor?"

Tulsidor didn't dare tell her.

"Well, whoever it was," she said, "I want him to come and teach here."

"You're sure about that?" said Tulsidor. "Absolutely sure?"

"Of course," said the teacher. She didn't know that it was the monster.

The following day there was panic in Jaisalmer, as Tulsidor walked down the main street holding onto one of the monster's fingers.

"Help!" they shouted. "We're all going to die! Somebody do something!"

"It's going to eat us up!" screamed an old lady. "It's going to have me for breakfast."

"Nonsense," said Tulsidor, "it's a vegetarian. Besides it's our new maths teacher, so you'd better get used to seeing it around."

And see it around they did, because the monster is still there, four hundred years later, teaching maths to all the little children of Jaisalmer, and teaching it rather better than anyone else in the world, I might add.

The Spaghetti Man

There is a shop in Venice that never opens. The white paint, which used to dazzle passers-by when the sun came out, is peeling off the walls. The blue gates that lead into the back yard are firmly bolted. Nobody knows what has become of Mr Fettucini, the man who used to run this pasta factory. And yet the place is not deserted. Once a year, in the absolute deadest part of night, the great, silver pasta machines can be heard as they grind into action. The following morning the blue gates creak open, a gleaming black van drives out and the pasta factory falls silent for another year.

In the kitchen Mrs King was having the usual problem.

"I hate it! Yeuch!"

"But you liked it yesterday, Timothy," said Mrs King.

"I did not," said Timothy rudely, "I've never liked it ever since before the day I was born."

"George," pleaded Mrs King. "Do something."

Mr King put down his paper and looked at Timothy. He had never been very good at telling his son off.

"Timothy," he said, "this is very bad form you know, old boy. Word to the wise. Do as the memsahib says or you'll find yourself doing a stretch in the cooler."

Timothy never understood what his father was talking about. It didn't sound like a telling off so he started screaming again.

"I hate your cooking. Your food smells disgusting. It makes me want to be SICK!"

Mrs King left the kitchen in tears, Mr King left the kitchen for work and Timothy left the kitchen in a mess.

Timothy was a rude little boy. Even his friends said so and none of them were saints. He was nice enough when he was playing, or having a bath, but come mealtimes he turned into a hideous, squealing, moaning monster, who spat his food over the walls and hurled abuse at his poor mother. He was, in short, revolting. A spoilt brat who needed to be taught a lesson.

It was a Sunday when Timothy got his first visit. Mrs King had spent the whole morning in the kitchen preparing a Sunday roast. Timothy had been out with his father to watch a polo match in Richmond Park and he was bored silly.

"I don't want that muck," he said. "Give me fish fingers, chips and peas."

"Hold fire, lad, hold fire!" whispered Mr King, but Timothy was in no mood to hold fire. He shut his eyes tight and held his breath.

"Your food won't go away just because you've closed

22

your eyes, Timothy," said his mother.

"Then I shall make it go away," said Timothy and he picked up his plate and threw it at the sink. The food hit the window with a splat and slid down the glass into the goldfish bowl.

Timothy heard the latch click on the front door.

"Who's that?" said Mr King. There was no reply.

Timothy heard the creak of new leather, as a pair of heavy boots walked towards the kitchen across the wooden floor in the hall. Mrs King was too upset to have heard anything.

Timothy saw the long black shadow as it passed the light outside the cellar door.

"This is no time for jokes," shouted Mr King, rising from his chair nervously. "I was in the army, you know. Trained to kill and all that." Timothy saw the door handle twist violently just as Mr King pulled the door open.

There was nobody there.

Mr King went into the hall to investigate, and took Mrs King with him just in case there was any trouble. Timothy was left alone at the kitchen table. A paper napkin fell off the edge of the table as if somebody had just brushed past it, and Timothy thought that he could smell flour. No, he was sure he could smell flour. And baking. The sort of smell you get when you go out for a pizza. He hated pizza. He wanted to scream, but he couldn't. There was a hand over his mouth and the hairs on the back of his neck were standing on end. Something was scratching his cheek. No not something. Lots of things. Like long fingernails, only they weren't as thick as fingernails. They were more like sticks, or pins or . . . spaghetti. Spaghetti! That was the

smell! Then his parents came back into the room and the smell went away.

Much to his mother's surprise Timothy ate everything that was put in front of him for the next few days.

"Do you know what I think," said his mother one day.

"What?" said Timothy, tucking into his second yoghurt.

"I think we had a visit from the Spaghetti Man on Sunday."

"Who?" said Timothy reaching for a pear.

"The Spaghetti Man – he takes bad little children who won't eat their food to his factory in Italy, where he turns them into spaghetti. Have I never told you about him before?"

"Well, he didn't take me off to Italy, did he?"

"He's probably giving you a second chance," said Mrs King. "If you eat all your food from now on, he'll never come back."

Most children would have listened to what their mothers said. The threat of another visit from the Spaghetti Man would be enough to make them eat even sprouts, or cold rice pudding, or marmalade, without a word of complaint. Timothy, however, was a rare breed. Whatever his mother asked him to do, he'd always do the opposite. The very next morning things were back to normal.

"I want to go to the loo."

"Not in the middle of breakfast, Timothy."

"I'm not having breakfast," said Timothy.

"Yes you are," said his mother.

"No, I'm not, because this isn't breakfast. This is a cow pat," smirked Timothy, and he left the table without asking

to get down. Mr King was too busy reading his newspaper
to notice. Mrs King had had enough. She rushed out of
the kitchen and grabbed Timothy by the back of his shirt.
Then she frogmarched him back to the table, picked him
up, plonked him down and told him that he could sit there
all day for all she cared, until he had finished his toast.

Timothy did sit there all day. In fact, he sat there
all the next day as well. He tried hiding his toast in
the dustbin and pretending that he'd eaten it, but his
mother got it out again and put it back on his plate. He
tried feeding his toast to his goldfish, but they didn't like
it. He even tried slipping it into the postman's sack when
he delivered the letters, but the postman found it one street
later and posted it back through Timothy's letterbox. In
fact he tried everything to get rid of his toast, except eating
it.

On the morning of the third day Mr King went off to
work as usual and Mrs King went out for a walk. Normally
she would have taken Timothy, but he still hadn't eaten
his toast. This meant that Timothy was alone in the house
and he was furious. He went to the fridge and took out
everything inside. He put it all in a black plastic bin liner
and shoved it down the bottom of his mother's bed. Then
he kicked the cat. He found a large blue screwdriver that
belonged to his father and scratched his name across the
sitting room door. He filled his pockets with stones from
the garden and went around the house smashing lightbulbs
with them.

He was up in the bathroom putting the plug in the
bath and turning on the taps when he heard the latch
click on the front door. Good! His mother was back and

she'd be livid. He'd teach her to make him eat his toast! As the water rose in the bath he could hear the squeak of his mother's new leather boots as she walked across the wooden floor in the hall and climbed the stairs. As he turned the taps up to full power he saw his mother's shadow creep under the door. He laughed triumphantly as the first drop of water splashed over the edge and the door handle to the bathroom twisted violently. The door was flung open.

"See! I'm never eating toast again," shouted Timothy.

But he was shouting to himself, because there was nobody there. Just that smell again, of flour and baking . . . and spaghetti!

When Mrs King got home a couple of minutes later, the water was rushing down the stairs. She shouted for Timothy, but there was no reply.

Timothy awoke to find himself in a room full of children. All of them had grumpy looking faces, a bit like Timothy's. He wondered where on earth he was. He looked out of the window, but there was nothing to see, except a disused yard and two blue gates. Over in the corner a green tarpaulin had been thrown over a van, which Timothy could see was black.

"Where are we?" said Timothy to a girl with bright red curly hair.

"Have you never heard of the Spaghetti Man?" she said.

"What, that Italian geezer who turns children into pasta when they don't eat their food?"

"That's right," she said.

"But he's not real," said Timothy.

"Isn't he?" replied the curly haired girl. "Then what's this?" She showed Timothy a label on her coat. It read:

CURLY TWIRLS

"What are curly twirls?" said Timothy.

"They're those things you have with tomato sauce. That's what he's going to turn me into."

"You're fibbing me," said Timothy.

"Have a look at your own label, if you don't believe me," said the girl, and she wandered off.

Timothy's label was stitched onto his BMX sweat shirt. He read it upside down.

LASAGNE

"Yeuch!" thought Timothy. "Lasagne! Absolutely my all time worst food. Disgusting! Fancy being turned into lasagne when I don't even like it!"

He went around the room looking at everybody else's labels. Tall, thin children were marked up as spaghetti. The fat ones had Macaroni written all over them and the little kids were labelled as "Fasta Pasta". Timothy chuckled. He leapt onto a table.

"Listen everybody!" he shouted. "Stop looking so miserable. This is a joke. We're not going to be turned into pasta. The Spaghetti Man is just a story that our mums and dads made up to make us eat our food. I don't know about you, but I've had enough. I'm going home!"

He turned to the door, but a pair of new leather boots blocked his way. A man wearing a baker's apron and a chef's hat stood dusting the flour off his hands.

"Guess who I'm having for dinner tonight," laughed the Spaghetti Man. It was a cruel laugh that made the children suddenly wish they weren't there.

But, of course they were.

That night, as Venice slept peacefully, the great, silver pasta machines ground into action. In the morning a gleaming black van pulled away from the old pasta factory and the blue gates were bolted for another year.

Mr and Mrs King never saw their son Timothy again. Mrs King was rather pleased, although she never admitted it. He had been quite obnoxious. The worst behaved boy she had ever known. Mr King hadn't noticed that Timothy was missing. So Mrs King never told him.

Their lives went on pretty much as normal. Mr King would go off to work and Mrs King would stay at home and prepare his evening meal.

Tonight it's lasagne.

The Princess's Clothes

Once upon a time in a far away town called Crawley there lived a beautiful Princess. She wasn't really a princess, that just happened to be what her father called her.

"Come and give your daddy a cuddle, Princess," he would say. His Princess would then rise gracefully from her embroidered cushion, throw the picture book that she was reading into the fire, and go and sit on his lap. As he gently combed her shining red ringlets the Princess would smile sweetly, flutter her pretty little eyelashes and purr. "I do love you, Daddy."

"And I love *you*, Princess," he'd reply.

It was generally at about this point that the Royal goldfish would turn its face to the wall for fear of being sick.

One day a strange visitor came to the house. She had a long hard face, a mouth that looked as if she had a bad smell under her nose and a pointy chin with three black hairs on the end. She was dressed completely in black,

and under her arm she clutched a large crocodile skin briefcase.

"Felicity," (for this was the Princess's real name), "Felicity, this is Miss Shears," said Felicity's mother.

"She looks like a wicked witch," said Felicity, who always said the first thing that came into her head.

"Well she's not, are you, Miss Shears?"

"Oh dear me, no," said Miss Shears in a tiny, bird-like voice. "I'm not a *wicked* witch at all."

"Miss Shears is from the catalogue showroom. She's bought some pictures for you to look at."

"Don't like pictures!" sulked Felicity.

"Well, you'll like these," said her mother. "Miss Shears has brought them round specially. I want you to choose some new clothes."

"But Daddy always buys my clothes!" screamed Felicity, burying her head in a cushion, and bawling horribly until her tears made the pattern run on the sofa.

It was true. Ever since Felicity's mother could remember she had never been allowed to choose her daughter's clothes. Once a week, every Saturday morning, the King and his Princess would climb aboard their Royal Coach, ride into the centre of London and spend all day browsing through the most expensive fashion houses they could find.

Felicity's wardrobe was a sight for sore eyes. Pretty lace dresses embroidered with the wings of a thousand butterflies; pink, taffeta ball gowns with mother of pearl buttons; cashmere sweaters and matching silk head scarves; cotton pyjamas with silver twist waist bands; and knockabout dungarees made from the finest hand-spun gold thread. She had two hundred pairs of shoes; dancing shoes, party shoes, school shoes, knee length boots, ankle boots, high heels, low heels, sandals, slippers, slip ons, slip offs, sling backs, trainers and flip flops. And a collection of overcoats, capes and ponchoes that would make your eyes stick out on stalks.

She had the biggest and best collection of clothes in England. There had been articles written about her in *Vogue* and *Harpers and Queen*, and she had even appeared on television once, modelling a particularly beautiful tracksuit made out of dried rose petals and peanut shells.

Of course, paying all this attention to her clothes did not make Felicity the easiest of little girls to live with. She was never satisfied with what she had. She always wanted more. Why have one pair of suede gloves when twenty-five would do?

She picked and fussed her way through her wardrobe for hours every morning.

"I will *not* wear that pink flamingo belt with this black skirt. It doesn't match the ivory piping. I need something altogether nicer. Get me that grey moleskin one with the tortoiseshell buckle."

Her mother despaired. It was unnatural for a child to be so obsessed with how she dressed. She had to put a stop to this nonsense once and for all.

Miss Shears undid the clasp on her briefcase, and pulled out a large pile of magazines. The clasp was made from the head of a rattlesnake, and Felicity thought for a moment that she saw it move.

"Now, isn't that pretty, Felicity?" said her mother, pointing to a patchwork smock in one of the brochures.

"You'd look lovely in that."

"Shan't wear it," said Felicity.

"Or this denim dress. They're quite the rage now," added Miss Shears.

Felicity was already in a rage. "I don't like it. I don't like any of them. I only like pretty things, from pretty, expensive shops, that *I* can choose!"

"In that case," said her mother, "I shall choose for you."

Felicity jumped up off the sofa, knocked a lamp off the occasional table and stormed out of the room, slamming the door behind her.

Miss Shears sat with Felicity's mother for the rest of the morning. They looked at every picture on every page in every magazine and come lunchtime they had drawn up a long list of new clothes for Felicity.

"Goodbye, Felicity," called Miss Shears from the foot of the stairs as she prepared to leave. "See you very soon." Then she put on her black mackintosh and went out into the street. Felicity was watching from an upstairs window. She heard Miss Shears call up to her, she heard Miss Shears say thank you to her mother, she even heard Miss Shears shut the front door behind her, but when she looked to see Miss Shears leaving through the garden gate, Miss Shears wasn't there. She had vanished.

Felicity wouldn't talk to her mother for the next few days. When the parcel arrived from Miss Shears she went and hid in the garden shed.

"I'd rather live with spiders and beetles, than live with you!" she cursed. "I hate those clothes. I hate them. They make me look all fat and frumpy."

"You haven't even seen them yet," said her mother.

"Come inside and try them on."

Felicity refused to budge. She stayed in the garden shed until she fell asleep, when her father broke the window, unlocked the door and carried her upstairs to bed.

In the morning there was trouble. She woke up to find that her mother had completely rearranged her wardrobe. Gone were all her expensive designer clothes – they had been put in a top cupboard where she couldn't reach them. In their place were the most revolting looking things that Felicity had ever seen, and her mother was going to make her wear them.

"I don't like blue. I don't like green, and I *certainly* don't like turquoise!" she sobbed. In fact she didn't like the colour of any of her new clothes.

"You will go to school with no clothes on at all in a minute," said her mother.

"All right," she screamed, her little face turning purple with fury, "then I *will*! See if I care."

All her mother wanted was for Felicity to wear a pair of open-toed sandals with a blue "Fab Girl" mini skirt.

"Sandals are horrible!" she bellowed. "I want to wear my wellington boots!"

"It is summer, Felicity. Wellington boots will make your feet hot and sticky," said her mother, as calmly as she could.

"I want my feet to be hot and sticky!" replied Felicity. "They're my feet and I can do what I like with them."

"Then do it!" said her mother, who had had enough.

And so she did. Felicity changed completely, and came downstairs wearing a passion pink dressing gown, a flowery bath towel covered in bumble bees, held up by the shower attachment from the bath, three pairs of white bobby socks, red wellington boots, her father's old fishing hat and a fur coat that her mother had missed when she put all of Felicity's old clothes away . . .

"This is what I want to wear," said Felicity and she rushed out of the house to catch the school bus.

"Oh dear," said her father. "Wouldn't it be easier simply to throw her new clothes away."

"No it would not," said her mother.

"But she's my Princess, and Princesses are allowed to do what they want."

"She is a spoilt little madam," said her mother, "and she'll learn to do as she's told."

Felicity had a miserable day at school. Her choice of clothes had been a bad one. The fur coat itched, the wellington boots made her feet so hot that she thought she was melting, and, worst of all, children kept buzzing around her flowery bath towel, then coming up and sniffing the petals. Her mother had been right of course. Her mother always was, but Felicity was not going to let her know that. Instead she resolved to get rid of her new clothes that night.

As the clock struck eleven-thirty, Felicity opened her eyes. The room was pitch black. She lay in bed for a moment letting her eyes adjust to the light and running over the plan in her head. She would find the wrapping paper which the clothes had arrived in, repack the clothes and post them back to Miss Shears. That *horrible* Miss Shears who had been the cause of all her misfortune.

Felicity slipped quietly out of bed and tiptoed over to her

wardrobe. Slowly, she eased open the door, fearful lest the clothes should see what she was doing and call out. Good. They were all asleep. She went over to the wastepaper bin and pulled out the crumpled brown paper. As she laid it on her carpet and smoothed it out, something dropped to the floor. Felicity bent down and picked up a small black parcel which had the words "ONLY TO BE OPENED BY A PRINCESS" printed on it. She tore open the paper, and found to her surprise a tiny pair of silver sewing scissors. Attached to the handle was a note:

> "I've been sent by someone who
> Would like me to look after you.
> So treat me well, for all your days,
> If not, I'll make you mend your ways."

What a strange present, thought Felicity. Who could possibly have sent it to her?

She would probably have gone back to bed there and then to puzzle it out, if a second, more devious plan, had not suddenly sprung into her mind.

She pulled a patchwork smock out of the wardrobe, took the silver sewing scissors in her right hand and, very slowly, made a tiny snip in the sleeve. It was easy. The scissors cut through the material as if by magic. She cut again, faster this time, and the sleeve fell away onto the floor. Felicity was starting to enjoy herself. She pulled out more and more clothes. The scissors slashed through everything. They were cutting by themselves now. Ripping and tearing, shredding and snapping, until Felicity was surrounded by an enormous pile of rags that touched the ceiling.

"That'll teach that horrible old witch, Miss Shears," she laughed. "Now my mother will *have* to let me wear my old clothes!"

Then it happened. The scissors twisted in her hand and leapt out of her grasp.

"No!" shouted Felicity, but it was too late. The scissors had reached the top cupboard where all the Princess's clothes were stacked. She was helpless as the flashing blades tore her beloved clothes to shreds. The room became a whirlwind of silk, velvet, sequins and satin, which sucked Felicity into its centre and sent her spinning across the floor.

That was when she saw the face at the window. It was only there for a minute, but there was no mistaking the long hard face, the mouth that curled at the edges and the pointy chin with three black hairs on the end. It was Miss

Shears, sitting on a broomstick.

When her parents came into her room the following morning, they found Felicity's window wide open. Her wardrobe was empty. The clothes had all disappeared from the floor. Felicity was sitting in her bed, wrapped in a blanket.

"Princess!" said her father. "What has happened?"

"I'm not a Princess," said Felicity. "I'm Felicity and I haven't got any clothes to wear."

"Oh dear," said her mother.

"Oh sorry," said her father.

"Oh blast," said Felicity.

From that day on, Felicity went to school dressed in a blanket, and nothing else.

The Black Knight

Not so very long ago a good King ruled over the land of Ruritania. His name was Basil and he was much loved by his people. He treated them fairly and made sure that every family was well looked after. They had food and clothes·in abundance, and every Sunday was a day for celebration. They would dance and sing until sunset, and everybody was happy.

The day came, however, when King Basil died. There was much chaos and concern throughout the land, for he had died without having any children. There was no one to take over as King. The Prime Minister and all his advisors could not come up with a solution. As regrettable as it was, they had no choice, but to place an advertisement in the *Ruritania Herald*.

WANTED
Person of sound mind and pleasant disposition
to fill the vacancy for KING (or QUEEN) OF RURITANIA.
No time wasters please.

Many people applied for the job. Farmers from the east, business men from the west, a school teacher from the small town of Brossch and a newspaper owner who lived in the clouds on the top of a high mountain. But none was successful. They were all eminent people in their own fields, but to be a king (or queen) you have to be an eminent person in everybody else's field as well.

So it was that one year after King Basil's death, his successor had still not been appointed. The search continued deeper and deeper into the countryside for a suitable candidate, until the Prime Minister was sure that every single person in Rúritania had been given the chance to come forward. Yet still he had found no one who could match up to the late good King Basil.

It was about this time that the news of King Basil's death reached the neighbouring country of Draconia where Prince Egor, known as the Black Knight for his dreadful deeds on the battlefield, heard it with delight.

"Ruritania has no leader," he said to his generals. "To-morrow we shall gather up our armies, march across the border and seize their crown. If they cannot make up their minds, then I shall make them up for them. I shall be King of Ruritania."

"You will be the most powerful man in the world," said his Chief of Staff.

"Don't think I haven't thought of that!" said the Black Knight. "I shall also be the wealthiest man in the world, once I have stripped Ruritania of all its possessions." He laughed out loud, and his generals laughed with him.

The following day, the Black Army swept into Ruritania. It moved forward like a mighty column of ants, devouring everything in its path and leaving a trail of destruction behind it. The people of Ruritania were not prepared for such an onslaught and they put up little resistance. It was not long before the Black Knight and his generals had reached the great wall that surrounded King Basil's castle.

"We will camp here tonight!" shouted the Black Knight to his troops. "Rest now, for at dawn we will storm the castle!"

The Black Knight left his generals and went in search of a quiet retreat where he might construct a foolproof plan to capture King Basil's castle. He had not walked very far, when he chanced upon the River Alter. He had heard about this river. Its sparkling blue waters were renowned for their magic powers.

The Black Knight knelt down on the grassy bank, and was splashing his face with cool water when he noticed another face looking up at him from the river bed. "What a handsome fellow," he thought. Then he realised that it was his own reflection.

Suddenly, the face in the water came to life and spoke to him.

"Tomorrow morning may be too late, Black Knight. You have the most powerful army in the world. You are their most cunning General. You *will* smash Ruritania, you *will* seize its throne and you *will* be master of all its people . . . but only if you crush their armies tonight. Move under cover of darkness. Kill them all while they sleep in their beds!"

A baby pike was swimming underneath the Black Knight's reflection as it spoke and, thinking the reflection

was a tasty meal, it came to the surface and nibbled an ear. The clear water was dispersed into a thousand ripples, and before the pike could take a second bite, the Black Knight's reflection disappeared.

The Black Knight was furious. If that stupid pike had not been so nosey, he might have learnt a lot more from his reflection. Nonetheless, what little advice he had been given made good strategic sense. He would attack King Basil's castle that very night.

It was a bloody battle. Many of King Basil's loyal followers lost their lives in defence of the castle, but the might of the Black Army proved too strong. By morning the Black Knight had declared himself the new King of Ruritania. His reign of tyranny had begun, just as his reflection had predicted.

It was as if a dark cloud had settled over the country. People wept as their houses and possessions were taken away from them. Children were snatched from their mothers and put to work in the service of their new king. The Prime Minister and all his advisors were taken from their beds and hurled into the dungeons underneath the castle.

"Throw away the keys," ordered the Black Knight. "Let them rot down there for the rest of their short lives."

Singing and dancing were banned. Ruritania died.

The Black Knight enjoyed his new-found wealth and power. He could tell everyone what to do and no one dared to answer back. After a while, however, he grew weary of bullying people. Weeping peasants no longer interested him. He found the whole process of ruling a country rather boring. He needed some excitement.

He decided to return to the magic waters of the River Alter. He would ask his reflection for advice.

"You've given up!" said the reflection, staring up at the Black Knight from the murky water. "You're going soft. If you don't show these people who's boss, very soon they'll be telling *you* what to do."

A shadow squirmed between the rocks at the bottom of the river. A row of silver teeth flashed as the shadow changed direction and headed towards the surface.

"If you want people to go down on their knees to you," continued the reflection, "you must force them! Beat them, burn them, fry them alive in boiling oil!"

The pike that had once been a baby, but was now half grown, burst out of the water and with one snap of its vicious jaws, gobbled up the Black Knight's reflection, armour and all.

The Black Knight went back to King Basil's castle full of evil ideas. His reflection was right. He had to assert himself. So from that day on he ruled with a fist of iron. Anyone who dared to question him had his head chopped off. He had every piece of gold in the country brought to his castle and locked away in a strong room, to which only he had the key. He killed all the animals and burnt all the crops so that nobody had anything to eat. He declared that every single person in the country was his slave and he made them worship him.

He became like the devil and Ruritania was Hell.

A year passed, and the Black Knight was the most feared ruler in the whole world. Strangely though, the more powerful he became, the more frightened he became too, in case someone should rob him of his power. He needed someone to help him. He needed a friend to tell him what to do, but, of course he did not have any friends. Then he remembered his reflection.

He slipped out of the castle one morning and ran down to the banks of the River Alter. If anyone could advise him, his reflection could. He edged towards the muddy, brown water, and leant out, expecting to see his own face staring back at him, but there was nothing there. His reflection had disappeared.

Then something stirred in the depths. At first the Black Knight could not work out what was disturbing the water, but slowly he started to recognise his own features lying just below the surface. His reflection *had* returned. At least he thought it had. He peered closer. It was his face, all right, and yet it looked different. The face in the water was

grotesque. It was twisted. It was evil. Just then the Black Knight saw a fin break the water and he suddenly realised what he was staring at. The pike. The pike that was now fully grown. The pike that had swallowed his reflection. The pike that now had his face.

With one powerful thrust of its massive tail the great fish leapt from the water, its jaws gaping, its teeth flashing. It devoured the Black Knight in one bite.

Ruritania returned to normal from that day onwards. With the Black Knight dead, the Prime Minister was released from prison, and he set about appointing a new king (or queen) straight away. There were some people who wanted the pike to be king, because it had eaten the Black Knight, but fishes tend to make useless monarchs. Their crowns are forever slipping off, for one, and they put out a rather unattractive smell, for another. So it was never crowned.

Instead a young lady called Gertrude was chosen to be Queen. She ruled wisely and sensibly for many years, and gave the pike a special place in the Royal Goldfish pond, where it lived happily for the rest of its long life.

Glued to the Telly

Herbert Hinckley loves the television. He doesn't go to school. He doesn't go out to play. He doesn't have any friends. He doesn't need them, because Herbert Hinckley loves the television.

He sits all day in his shabby red armchair, eating packets of crisps and drinking Coca Cola. His parents don't seem to mind. So long as Herbert is happy, they are happy. So Herbert just sits there, day in day out, flicking between the channels, watching programme after mindless programme on a battered old television set.

If you ask Herbert what any of the programmes are about, he always replies, "Cheese and Onion." When Herbert watches the television, all he can think about is the flavour of his next packet of crisps.

The television set is as old as Herbert himself. His parents bought it for him on the day that he was born. It has seen better days. The back is held on with rubber bands and garden string. The knobs on the front have long since dropped off and been replaced by lumps of half-chewed bubble gum. The screen has got a crack across it, that Herbert mended with Sellotape and sticking plaster.

"Would you like to sleep down here tonight, Herbert, as a treat?" said his mother one day.

"Cheese and Onion," said Herbert.

"We thought you'd like to," said Mr Hinckley. "You can watch the television all night if you sleep down here."

"It'll make a nice change for you," said his mother, taking away the empty crisp packets, and pushing a fresh bag into Herbert's lap.

Although you'd never have known it, Herbert was very excited as his parents made up the sofa in the sitting room.

"Sleep well, dear," said Mrs Hinckley.

"Salt and Vinegar," said Herbert, who was obviously enjoying himself, because the last time he had asked for Salt and Vinegar, England were winning a test match

49

against the West Indies.

Herbert sat in his armchair until the little white dot disappeared from the screen. Then he got up and switched the television off at the mains. It was an old set, so this was a wise precaution. He didn't want any fires starting while he was asleep. He looked at the newspaper to check what time the Breakfast Show started, set his alarm, and climbed into bed, exhausted after a hard day's watching.

He dreamt of cheese and onion crisps.

An hour later, while Herbert slept, a silver grey cloud passed between the moon and Herbert's house. The sitting room was plunged into darkness. A streak of lightning cracked through the sky and struck the aerial that led directly into the back of Herbert's television. A switch clicked on. A faint humming sound grew from deep inside the belly of the machine. Then suddenly, BLIP! The television switched itself on. The little white dot that had been no bigger than a fingernail started to grow, getting larger and larger with every sleepy breath that Herbert took. It was as if Herbert and the television were breathing as one. The dot filled the screen and spread out into the room. It crept across the floor towards the sofa, edged over Herbert's pillow and onto his face. Herbert half opened one eye, but it was too late. The blinding light had completely surrounded him and suddenly, like a fisherman's net, it snatched him up and dragged him back through the television screen.

"Good morning, Herbert," said Mrs Hinckley when she came downstairs the next morning. "Crisps for breakfast?" She stopped at the door to the sitting room. "Herbert?" She went in and looked behind the curtains. "Herbert?" Mr and Mrs Hinckley could not find Herbert anywhere.

"He's probably turned into a television set!" laughed Mr Hinckley.

"That's not funny, George," said his wife, but she peered into the television screen just in case.

Herbert got the shock of his life when he opened his eyes and saw his mother's face pressed up against the outside of the screen. She looked like a giant goldfish, only goldfish didn't have bad teeth and a big nose.

"Cheese and Onion!" he said to her, but she couldn't hear him. In fact she couldn't see him either, because he was only six inches tall. He was all alone inside his own television set.

It was very dark, except for a flashing red light at the end of a narrow passage. His way forward was blocked by a big metal coil that hummed like a top. When Herbert tried to pick it up, it burnt his hand. He lay down on the floor, braced himself against an electrical circuit board and kicked the coil as hard as he could. It snapped off and shot a jagged blue spark into the ceiling, where it fizzed and crackled. Then he rolled over and crawled up the passageway towards the flashing light.

As he got closer he saw a door. He could hear a voice as well, which was strangely familiar. It was as if he'd heard it once in a dream. He eased down the door handle and slipped into the room.

Inside there was a lady, sitting behind a desk. She was shuffling and re-shuffling thousands of bits of paper. She turned towards Herbert as he came in, and he instantly recognised her. It was Gayna Honeycombe, his all-time favourite newsreader! But what was she doing talking to herself?

"The mystery of disappearing television addict, Herbert Hinckley, continues today."

Herbert's ears nearly dropped off the side of his head. Gorgeous Gayna was talking about him!

"His parents have expressed concern for his health. They are worried that he won't be able to find enough packets of Cheese and Onion crisps to keep his strength up. Apparently, Herbert likes to eat at least fifty packets a day. And now the main points of the News again . . ."

Herbert was in love and he didn't care who knew it. The gentle waft of Gayna's perfume had sent his love buds into frantic activity. His mouth was drooling. His arms were outstretched. He ran towards his screen goddess calling out her name for all the world to hear.

And she ignored him.

She never once looked up. In fact she went one further than that. As Herbert threw himself across the desk into her arms, she vanished. She completely disappeared, along with the desk and her bits of paper.

"How very odd," thought Herbert. It was just as if somebody had switched Gayna off. Well, somebody had – Herbert's mother. She wanted to watch the Cowboy film on the other side.

Suddenly, an electric cable snapped off the panel above Herbert's head, and crashed down into a bank of green bulbs, sending a shower of glass all over him. The cable thrashed wildly like a dying fish, then it was still.

Herbert gulped. The old television set was collapsing under his extra weight. He ran into a rusty corridor. Puddles of deadly acid oozed up from beneath the metal floor, and lumps of solder dangled precariously from the

ceiling like so many dead spiders. The inside of Herbert's television was a mess. He had to get out of there.

There were hundreds of doors in the corridor. Herbert opened one. A little girl and a clown were sitting in the corner, listening to horrible, soupy music on an old gramophone.

"Get out," said the little girl. "Can't you see we're playing noughts and crosses?"

"Cheese and Onion," said Herbert. What he meant to say was sorry. He backed out and tried the next room along.

As he opened the door, a bullet whistled past his nose and buried itself into the wall behind his left ear. A heavy fist thumped him on the end of his chin, and a large pair of hands picked him up and flung him halfway across the room.

"Howdy stranger," said the bartender. "Enjoying the fight?"

Herbert was still slightly dazed as he looked up. He was in a Wild West saloon bar, in the middle of the roughest, toughest brawl he had ever seen. The bartender ducked as a bottle smashed into the mirror behind him.

"What you having, pardner?" he said to Herbert. "Whisky?"

"A packet of Cheese and Onion crisps, please," replied Herbert. He was famished.

A very large, hairy man suddenly appeared next to him. "I'm going to hit you with my sledgehammer," he said. "Would you like that?"

Herbert dived behind the bar as the large hairy man turned a perfectly nice bar stool into matchwood.

"It gets worse every night," said the little orange bear, who was also taking cover behind the bar. His doggy friend squeaked in agreement. "I mean why do they have to hurt each other? By the way I'm Sooty," said the bear, "and this is my friend Sweep."

"Pleased to meet you," said Herbert. "I'm Herbert Hinckley. I'm a great fan of yours. I've seen all your films. What are you doing behind this bar?"

"We're waiting to do our show," said Sooty wearily. "We can't start until they've finished fighting. Our viewers will be furious, you know. They want water pistols, not guns. They want to see custard pies pushed in people's faces, not chairs broken over some poor fellow's back. I mean look . . ." Sooty picked up a tiny chair and smashed it over Herbert's head. ". . . that's just not funny, is it?" said Sooty.

"No," said Herbert, "not really." Then his eyes rolled upwards and he crashed to the floor. Sooty had knocked him out.

When he came to, Herbert's arms appeared to be trapped by his side, but upon opening his eyes, he discovered that he was tucked up in a hospital bed. A doctor and a nurse were standing over him and gazing at each other.

"Nurse Pagett," said the doctor.

"Yes, Dr Miles," replied the nurse with a tear in her eye.

"The whole world thinks we're mad," said the doctor, "but we're not. I can't help myself, but I love you, Nurse Pagett."

"And I love you, Dr Miles!" she sobbed.

"Please, call me Tim," said the Doctor.

Herbert didn't know where to look as Doctor Miles and Nurse Pagett threw their arms around each other and started kissing. It was like a scene out of one of those terrible television soap operas.

In fact it was one of those terrible television soap operas. That was why everyone had an Australian accent.

The door burst open and a woman rushed in. She was also crying. "I'm the boy's mother!" she wept.

She didn't look anything like Herbert's mother. "Is my son going to live?"

The doctor put the nurse down and put his arms round this strange woman instead.

"Sit down," he said (now there were tears in his eyes). "I'm afraid your son will never recover."

"Never recover!" shouted Herbert sitting up in bed. "I feel fine! I wouldn't mind a packet of Cheese and Onion crisps, but otherwise I've never felt better."

"But that's the problem!" said the doctor, turning to Herbert for the first time. "It is an absolute medical certainty that by six o'clock tomorrow morning, you will be a fully fried up Cheese and Onion crisp!"

"What!" shouted Herbert.

"Look at your fingernails," said the doctor. "They've already gone brown and crispy. Try one."

Herbert nibbled his thumb nail and screamed. It tasted just like a Cheese and Onion crisp. Delicious. He took a second bite, then suddenly leapt from his bed.

"What am I doing?" he shouted. "I'm eating myself!"

He was going to turn into his favourite food by the morning. How could he stop himself from eating himself all up? More to the point, how could he stop himself from

56

turning into a crisp.

"Where are you going?" shouted the doctor, as Herbert crunched his way over to the door. He had one plan. Find a shower and stand underneath it all night. One thing that crisps weren't, was soggy. If he could keep himself soaking wet all night he couldn't possibly be a crisp, and if he wasn't a crisp there was no danger of him dying from being eaten by himself.

Herbert rushed from his hospital room and found himself back in the rusty corridor. As he ran in search of water, he tripped and fell against a metal grille. A tangle of red and green cables spilled out into a quivering heap on the floor. Sparks exploded from the cables and lit a circle of small fires.

Mr and Mrs Hinckley were still in the sitting room watching the television.

"I've seen enough of this hospital rubbish now," said Mrs Hinckley. "Let's turn over and watch the cookery programme on the other side. The one with that fat chef."

"Yes. I like him," said Mr Hinckley. "He's very funny." Then, "It's a shame Herbert's not here to see it."

They switched channels and didn't notice the thin plume of smoke that had started to rise from the back of the television.

Herbert was still looking for a shower room, but it was getting more and more difficult to see where he was going as smoke billowed into the corridor. Shadowy figures rushed past in the opposite direction, shouting: "Fire! Fire! Get out before it's too late! Women, children and puppets first!"

"Stop!" shouted Herbert. "I need to find water before

I turn into a Cheese and Onion crisp."

But nobody was listening. Even Batman and Robin ran past and pretended not to hear.

Mr and Mrs Hinckley had turned over to the cookery programme. The fat cook was showing everyone how to make potato crisps.

"Mmmm," said Mrs Hinckley. "Those look so good I can almost smell them!"

The smoke was now rising steadily from the back of Herbert's television, and filling the room.

Herbert was banging on the back of the television screen. "Help!" he shouted.

He could see his parents sitting on the sofa, sniffing the air.

"Did you hear anything just then?" said Mr Hinckley.

"It was the cat," said his wife.

"I'm in the telly!" cried Herbert.

"Could you please get out of my way," said the fat cook, who was standing behind Herbert in the kitchen. "People can't see what I'm doing."

"Tell them!" pleaded Herbert. "Tell them I'm in the television, there's smoke coming out the back, and I'm going to be turned into a Cheese and Onion crisp! They can't hear me."

The cook was not only fat, he was also mad. "You have smoke coming out of your back and you're a Cheese and Onion crisp?"

"No. I'm going to become a Cheese and Onion crisp!"

"If that's what you want," said the chef, picking Herbert up by the seat of his trousers, "why wait? Be a Cheese and Onion crisp now!" He opened the oven door and slid

Herbert in.

Mr and Mrs Hinckley were laughing so much that they did not see the first flame leap out of the television set.

"That chef is so funny!" gasped Mr Hinckley. "Did you notice when he put that extra large potato into the oven?"

"It looked just like Herbert!" screamed Mrs Hinckley as she held her sides and went red in the face. "Oh look," she went on, pointing to the fire, which was now blazing out of the back of the television, "that chef is burning the crisps!"

Mr and Mrs Hinckley clutched each other, fell off the sofa and rolled around the carpet in a state of helpless hysteria. They were laughing so much that they never heard Herbert's cries for help.

When they stopped laughing, the television had gone. It had burnt away to a pile of ashes. Sitting on the top was a big, fat Cheese and Onion crisp.

"Look at this mess," said Mrs Hinckley. "Whatever will Herbert say when he sees what's happened to his television set?"

"I'll buy him another one," said Mr Hinckley. "This one was getting a bit old anyway."

"I wonder where Herbert is?" said his mother, unwinding the flex to the Vacuum Cleaner.

"Probably gone out," said his father.

Mrs Hinckley started hoovering up the pile of ashes. "Well, he can't have gone far," she said. "He's left a crisp behind." She nibbled a corner. "Cheese and Onion. His favourite. I've never known him leave a Cheese and

Onion. He's bound to come back to finish it."

She picked the crisp up, sealed it in a tupperware box, put it in the fridge and, unfortunately, forgot all about it.

The Barber of Civil

You will probably have heard of a town called Saucy by Sea. The children who lived in the town had a terrible reputation. They were the rudest children in the world. Parents were often to be seen crying in the streets as their sons and daughters shouted abuse at them. It was an appalling sight that made visitors to the town shudder with horror, and nobody knew what to do about it.

One day a new shop appeared in the High Street. The sign outside said "BARBER". Then in small letters underneath: *Children a Speciality*. The window was permanently steamed up so that nobody could see in from the street. Little drops of water ran down a neat, handwritten notice hanging in the door.

THREE CUTS:
SHORT BACK AND SIDES, PUDDING BASIN
or THE FULL CHOP.

The barber was a cheerful looking man, with a handlebar moustache and bright red cheeks. He visited the local schools and offered free hair cuts to all the children. He very quickly became popular. This was not because he was a particularly good barber (in fact many of the parents noticed that their children's hair was exactly the same length when they came out as it was when they went in), but because the foul children of Saucy by Sea miraculously changed whenever they visited his shop. They would go in cheeky and rude, and come out as polite as polite could be.

However, there were two things about the new barber that people considered strange. Firstly, he never allowed parents into his shop. Children had to go in alone. Secondly, he had a very nasty collection of grey slugs, which he kept in a large glass jar by the cash till. But, seeing as he provided such an excellent service, the parents of Saucy by Sea were happy to allow him these two eccentricities.

A new family moved into the town. The two children, Tania and Peregrine, started at the local school in the Autumn, and it soon became clear that they were not fitting in.

"Can anyone tell me what two and two is?" said Peregrine's maths teacher.

"Two. Two," shouted Peregrine, without putting his hand up. "It's what a ballerina wears, isn't it? A tutu."

"Put your hand up when you have something sensible to say, Peregrine," said the teacher.

Peregrine put his hand up.

> "Jingle Bells
> Teacher Smells
> I wish she'd go away.
> She looks just like an elephant
> I've nothing more to say."

There was a gasp from the class. Nobody would dare to be so cheeky to a teacher. Peregrine sat back in his chair and grinned. The teacher was bright red. It was all she could do to control her fury.

"Go and see the headmaster!" she said, slowly. "Now!"

Tania, meanwhile, was doing gym.

"Tuck your skirt into your knickers yourself!" she shouted at her games teacher. "I'm not doing it."

"Tania, I'm not going to argue with you. Everyone does gym in their knickers."

"Not me!" Tania said. "I've got a note from my mum."

"Let me see it then," said the games teacher.

"All right!" said Tania defiantly. Then she jumped on top of a bench, opened her mouth and sang in her loudest voice, "Laaaaaaaaaaaaaaaaaaaaaaaaaaaaaaaaaaaaaaaaaaaa!"

There was a stunned silence from the rest of the class. Tania jumped down off the bench. "It's a musical note. My mum's always singing it!"

The games teacher took a deep breath. "Go and see the headmaster," she said, slowly. "Now!"

The headmaster was an old man who had been in the teaching business all his life. He knew exactly how to deal with cheeky children. Leave them outside his office for a while until they were really scared, then call them in with a voice like thunder. Stand them in front of his desk, while he faced the window, flexing a long bamboo cane in his hands. Then turn and confront the offenders. Crack the cane down on the desk in front of them, and roar, "Well? What have you got to say for yourselves?"

It always worked. The children were always deeply ashamed about their behaviour and always said sorry.

Tania and Peregrine had been waiting in the corridor for about ten minutes when the headmaster called them in. He was standing by the window, playing with a large stick. They stood by his desk, waiting for him to say something. Then suddenly he turned round and thumped the stick down on the desk in front of them.

"Well?" boomed the headmaster. "What have you got to say for yourselves?"

Tania and Peregrine looked at each other and shrugged their shoulders. Then they started singing:

"We're not scared of your stupid old stick,

If you really want to know, you make us sick.
'Cos you look like a camel with a hairy hump,
You're a ninny, you're a twit, you're a great fat lump."

There was a dull thud as the headmaster collapsed behind his desk. Tania and Peregrine waited. A hand appeared over the telephone, then a white face.

"Could you get Matron, please," murmured the headmaster, for whom the song had obviously been a big shock. "Then kindly leave my office."

The next day was Friday. Friday was the day that the barber came to the school to find new customers. The first class he visited was Peregrine's.

"Good morning, class," said the barber.

"Good morning, sir," replied everyone except Peregrine. The barber put on his spectacles and stared at him.

"Don't you want to say good morning to me?" said the barber.

"No," said Peregrine rudely. "I'd rather say goodbye."

The barber chuckled. "You look like you need a hair cut, young man. Come and see me tomorrow morning." Then he took out a pencil and wrote SHORT BACK AND SIDES in a little black book.

The barber entered Tania's class just as she was flicking ink pellets at the teacher, who had her back turned and was writing French words on the blackboard. The class stood up when they saw the barber come in. Tania went one further. She stood on the top of her desk, stuck her tongue out and waggled her fingers in her ears. The barber took out his little black book.

"And what might your name be?" he said to Tania.

"It might be Queen Elizabeth the first or Madonna, but it isn't!" she replied.

"It's Tania Windsor," said the teacher.

The barber wrote the name down.

"Tania," he said, "I think you need a hair cut as well. Come to my shop tomorrow morning with Peregrine and I'll see what I can do for you."

The following morning Tania and Peregrine turned up at the barber's shop for their haircuts. A bell rang in the distance as they pushed open the door. They were in a small room with shiny red lino on the floor. In the middle stood a large black and chrome dentist's chair underneath a bright overhead light. A bag of steel instruments sat on a shelf to the left of the chair and a black cat lay asleep next to it. Strangely, there were no mirrors. Perhaps the barber didn't want his customers to see what he was doing.

"He's not here," said Tania. "He's forgotten we're coming."

Peregrine sidled up to the cash till. "Look at these!" he shouted, lifting the barber's collection of grey slugs down off the counter.

"Imagine putting one of those in your mouth!" squealed Tania. "Oh no, Peregrine. No, don't!"

Peregrine had unscrewed the lid of the jar, fished out a slug and was pretending to eat it.

"I'll be sick!" screamed Tania.

"So will he," said a voice from the back of the shop. Peregrine got such a fright that he swallowed the slug he was playing with, and dropped the jar on the floor. The glass smashed and a heaving, twisting ball of slimy grey slugs spilled out onto the floor. As they slithered around

Tania's feet she heard a hundred different voices shout out:

"Shan't!" "Won't do it!" "Don't care." "And I hate you too!"

"Get them off me!" she shrieked.

The barber bent down, scooped up the chattering slugs and squeezed them into his pocket.

"You shouldn't play with other people's property," he said.

"Well, you shouldn't leave them where I can reach them," replied Peregrine cheekily.

"You think you're really clever, don't you?" said the barber.

"Well, you're certainly not," said Peregrine, "otherwise your best friends wouldn't be slugs."

The barber laughed. "Those aren't slugs."

"Yes they are," said Tania. "Aren't they?"

The barber said nothing.

"Well, if they're not slugs, what are they then?"

The barber simply smiled and locked the door. "Now we won't be disturbed," he said.

He tied a small plastic bib around each of their necks and went over to his tool bag. Peregrine and Tania watched him closely as he took out a silver razor. He ran his tongue down the edge of the blade to test how sharp it was. A thin red line of blood appeared on his tongue, which he promptly swallowed.

The children were more than a little frightened. Nobody had ever cut their hair with a razor blade before.

"Who wants to be first?" he asked, taking out his little black book. "Peregrine, with your short back and sides, or Tania? I have you down for the full chop."

"But I don't want all my hair chopped off," she said.

"We'll start with Peregrine, then. Up you come!"

The barber helped Peregrine into the black and chrome dentist's chair. He pressed a lever and the chair flattened out, so that Peregrine was lying on his back looking up into the overhead light. The barber tied two leather straps around Peregrine's wrists.

"Now, open wide!" he said.

Tania screamed. "Stop! You're not a dentist. Why should he open his mouth? You cut people's hair."

"Whatever gave you that idea," he laughed. "I teach little children to keep a civil tongue in their heads."

"What *do* you cut then?" asked Tania, nervously.

"I'll give you one guess," said the barber, sticking his tongue out at her. Peregrine gasped.

"So those aren't slugs in your pocket?"

"No! Of course not!" shouted the barber. "They're children's tongues. The little bits of children's tongues that make you all so foul mouthed. I snip out the rudeness. I trim off the cheekiness. I cut away the bad language, and when I've finished I rinse your mouths out with soap and water."

When Tania and Peregrine went back to school on Monday, they were different children. Their tongues were shorter for one. Also, they didn't swear, they weren't cheeky and they didn't try to be clever in front of the rest of the class. In fact they were two of the politest children in a school with a growing reputation for being the politest school in the world.

The barber left Saucy by Sea that week and was never seen again. He went off in search of other children in other towns. So if a new barber arrives at your school, and his pockets are bulging with slugs, I suggest you keep your mouth firmly shut and only speak when you're spoken to.

The Man with a Chip on his Shoulder

One day a man woke up and there was a huge chip on his shoulder.

"Typical," he moaned, "it always happens to me."

The End.

The Giant Who grew too Big for His Boots

Not so long ago, there lived a giant called Hugh, who lived in a tiny cottage in Wales. He was known as Huge Hugh, because his hands were the size of dustbin lids and his feet were as long as a pair of skis. He had a mop of tangly black hair on top of his head, and another mop of tangly black hair growing off his chin. What was left of his face was covered in warts. His tongue was purple and swollen from all the eating that he did, and when he talked, it stuck out between his lips and sprayed the room with spittle from ceiling to floor.

His wife used to carry an umbrella to keep herself dry. Hugh was always shouting at her and the walls of their cottage were permanently wet.

"Fetch me a cow thsandwich," he would dribble, "or else I'll thsit on top of you and turn you into meat paste."

Huge Hugh was a big bully with an enormous appetite.

One morning, after a light breakfast of twenty-seven buckets of cereal, fourteen apple trees and a bathful of

72

tea, Hugh leaned back in his chair and roared, "I need more thspace!" His wife didn't get her umbrella up in time and got soaked.

"Why?" she said, drying herself with a tea towel.

"Because this cottage isn't big enough!" shouted Hugh. "When I take a bath my toes thstick up the plugs. When I eat at the kitchen table my elbows knock the china off the thsideboard and I can't get into the toilet! I need more thspace!"

Huge Hugh left the cottage in a rush, banging his head on the back door as he went.

He stood outside his neighbour's house and shouted, "Mr Thsparrow!" for that was his neighbour's name. A timid little man wearing gumboots and a woolly hat appeared round the side of the house.

"Yes," he said. Hugh looked down at this weedy specimen.

"Are you ThSparrow?" said Hugh.

Mr Sparrow ducked and ran for cover as Hugh's spittle shot from his mouth like bullets from a machine gun.

"Yes," replied a distant voice.

"Thsuper," said Hugh. "I'm Huge Hugh and unlessth you give me your houthse, I'll stand here all day and thsay a lot of things beginning with 's'."

"If you do that, you'll spit my house down," said the distant voice.

"Exactly," said Hugh. Then he started:

"Thshe thsells thsea thshells on the thsea thshore. The thsea thshells that thshe thsells are thsea thshells for thsure . . ."

Seconds later Mr Sparrow and his family waded out

of the back door wearing mackintoshes and sou'westers.

Hugh moved in directly they had gone. He threw all their furniture into the road to make more space and went to sleep in the large room downstairs. It hadn't been a large room before Hugh moved in. In fact it had been the sitting room, dining room, kitchen, playroom and study. Hugh had simply knocked a couple of walls down.

When he woke up something very strange had happened. He had grown bigger. His head had swelled to ten times its normal size and was poking through the roof. His legs were sticking out of the windows and his feet were now as long as railway carriages.

"I need more thspace," roared Hugh. A thin spray of spittle squirted skyward from his mouth.

In a nearby village a freak rainstorm swept down the high street, soaking everything in its path. It lasted for fifteen seconds and ruined everybody's washing.

Hugh wiped his lips, brushed the chimney pot off his nose and looked around for somewhere bigger to stay.

In the distance, behind a long line of trees, a thin, trail of white smoke snaked up into the sky. Forgetting that he was still inside Mr Sparrow's house, Hugh stood up. The house was torn from its foundations and clung to Hugh's chest and arms like a brick coloured waistcoat. Beyond the trees he could see two villages perched on top of two hills.

"Mine!" thought Huge Hugh. He stepped over the trees and approached the villages.

The streets were deserted. He couldn't see any sign of life.

Hugh laughed out loud. "Too thscared to face me, eh?"

A little voice spoke up from somewhere near Hugh's knees. "If you have to shout, then go and do it somewhere else!"

"Who thsaid that?" said Hugh, showering the surrounding fields of wheat.

"I did!" said the voice again. "Down here!"

Hugh knelt down and came face to face with an angry vicar, who was hanging out of the church belfry.

"I am trying to conduct a service for these good village folk," said the vicar.

"Well, *I* am trying to find somewhere to thsleep," said Hugh putting his nose next to the Vicar's head and spraying him clean out of the bell tower.

"Shove off, Hugh," shouted the villagers from inside the church. Hugh peeled off the roof and put his eye close up to the congregation. "Thshove off yourselves!" he spat.

The villagers swam to safety. Hugh had found somewhere warm to spend the night.

Hugh wriggled into the two town halls, laid his head on a municipal library and kept his toes warm by putting each of them into a separate greenhouse. There was plenty of room in two whole villages for him to get comfy. In the middle of the night however he woke up with a start. He was freezing. It felt as if somebody had pulled the cover off him. Hugh opened an eye. He could see the stars. He opened the other eye. There was the moon. He had grown again. His head was higher than the clouds and the two villages were clustered round his ankles like a pair of unlaced boots.

"I need more thspace!" roared Hugh. A huge spray of spittle shot skywards from his mouth.

In nearby Scotland a freak rainstorm swept the length

and breadth of the country, soaking everything in its path. It lasted for three minutes and ruined everybody's hairdos.

Hugh wiped his lips and looked around him for somewhere bigger to stay. In the distance, at the end of a long straight road, a pocket of bright lights beckoned.

Hugh took over the City of London. He sprawled in Hyde Park. He drank water from the Thames. He ate pigeons by the handful from Trafalgar Square. No sooner had he claimed the city as his own, however, than he grew again, and every time he got bigger he needed more space. After London, it was Bristol, then Manchester, Liverpool, Hull and Edinburgh. By the time he had a toe in Ireland, Hugh was six hundred miles high.

Still he kept growing. Still he kept roaring, "I need more thspace!"

Still he kept spraying. Great Britain was having the wettest April in living memory. People were trading their cars in for luxury yachts and rowing boats.

The President of the United States of America phoned Huge Hugh up.

"Hugh," he said, "Hugh, baby. I hear you want to move into America."

"That's right," replied Hugh, "in a big way."

"Well, excuse me, Hugh," said the President nervously, "but I have to warn you, that you take one step towards the United States, and I'll be forced to send aeroplanes and rockets after you, to knock you out the sky."

Hugh laughed and slammed the receiver down. When you're as big as a country you don't have to listen to anyone.

After a quick snack of three thousand sheep and four

fields of carrots, Hugh took a couple of paces to the right and crossed the Atlantic Ocean as if it were no bigger than a puddle. True to his word, the American president sent up every aeroplane and rocket in his possession. Hugh ate them all for pudding.

"I need more thspace," roared Hugh. An absolutely enormous spray of spittle gushed skyward from his mouth.

In nearby Africa a freak rainstorm swept the length and breadth of the continent, soaking everything in its path. It lasted for six hours and ruined everybody's crops.

Hugh wiped his lips and looked around him for somewhere bigger to stay.

The rest of the world was very nervous. Hugh was growing at such an alarming rate, that he was no longer Huge Hugh, he was Absolutely Ginormous, Towering, Can't-see-his-head-for-the-clouds Hugh. When he went to sleep at night, he put his feet in Australia, his bottom in India and his head on a light pillow of snow in Antarctica. He spanned the globe. There wasn't a part of the earth that didn't belong to him.

After a fortnight of almost constant growing, and spittle spraying, Hugh found himself in the farthest corner of the Universe. He had outgrown the moon and the sun. He had rocketed past Mars and Jupiter. He had eaten the Milky Way on his way through. He was all alone, millions and millions of miles from home.

"I need more thspace!" roared Hugh, but there was no more space. He had taken every little bit of space going in the whole galaxy and beyond.

Then he had a visitor. An unmanned satellite had been sent up from Earth. It buzzed around Hugh's nose and annoyed him.

"Are you Huge Hugh?" said the computer on the satellite.

"No, I'm Everything in the Universe Hugh and I need more thspace!" said Hugh.

"Do stop saying that," said the satellite.

"What?" said Hugh.

"I need more space," replied the satellite.

"Do you?" said Hugh. "Thso do I."

"No. We'd like you to stop saying it."

"Why?" said Hugh.

"Because every time you do, you spray the entire Universe and it rains non-stop on earth for five days. People are going mad down there. They're scared of drowning."

"What do I care?" said Hugh. "Let them drown. I need more thspace!"

Then he grabbed the satellite before it could escape. "I'm going to eat you now," said Hugh.

"I wouldn't do that," said the satellite, "I'm covered in spiky aerials. If you bite on one of them a great big wind bag like you is going to burst."

"A great big wind bag! I'll show you who's a great big wind bag!" said Hugh, and he popped the satellite, which was no bigger than a Maltezer, into his mouth. He chewed for a moment and then suddenly, POP! One of the satellite's aerials pricked Hugh's tongue.

Like an enormous balloon losing all its air, Huge Hugh shrivelled and shrank his way back down to Earth. Back past the stars; back through the clouds; back to where he had once lived with his poor, long-suffering wife.

When he had stopped getting smaller he was no bigger than a matchstick.

It was raining hard as Hugh picked himself out of the

mud. He was soaked through. He needed to find some-where warm and dry to sleep. He stood on a mushroom to get a better view and saw a snail grazing lazily on a nearby leaf. Hugh jumped off his mushroom and pushed his way through the grass. He pulled himself up to his full height, of nearly two inches, and said, "I'm Huge Hugh."

"Really," said the snail, who was not interested.

"I need more thspace," squeaked Hugh.

The snail wiped his eye, where Hugh had spat.

"I want that house on your back."

"Really?" said the snail. "So do I." Then he slid up to Hugh and slimed all over him.

"Oh," said Teeny Tiny Hugh, as he lay on the grass unable to move for snail's jelly.

He never asked for more space again.

The weather got better too.

The Wooden Hill

The boy's name was Jack. Jack was bored. He wanted his mum to read him a bedtime story, but she was busy reading her newspaper.

"Mum," said Jack, lying across the sofa and putting his head in her lap, "what are you reading?"

His mum ignored him. From where he was lying, Jack could see right up her nose. He reached up and stuck his finger in her left nostril. "You've got long black hairs in your nose," he said.

"What is the matter with you, Jack?" she snapped, leaping up with the pain and plonking Jack off her lap onto the floor.

"Will you read me a story?" said Jack.

"Later," said his mum, "when I've finished the crossword."

Jack rolled onto his back and sighed deeply. "She's a real old dragon, my mum," he thought, feeling frightfully sorry for himself. As a matter of fact he could just imagine her as a dragon. Green spiky hair, wings tucked away under her cardigan, teeth ready-sharpened to bite his head off. He wouldn't want her to kiss him goodnight, though. Ugh! She'd burn his lips off! Jack snorted and laughed out loud.

"Jack! Please! I'm trying to concentrate!"

"But I want a book!"

"Then go upstairs and get one," said his mum.

"But you've got longer legs," whined Jack. "Mine are much shorter and get tired. You do it!"

Jack's mum put her paper down, and looked at him wearily. "Jack, you are nearly five years old. Don't be silly. If you want me to read you a book, you can go and get one from your bedroom." And that was her final word.

The real reason that Jack did not want to go upstairs by himself was simple. He was afraid of the dark. It was too spooky. He had tried it once before, but he hadn't made it past the umbrella stand in the hall. No, he wouldn't do it. His mum would have to go for him.

He tried to attract her attention by tapping his foot against the coffee table in an annoying sort of way, but she didn't even blink. He rolled up bits of carpet fluff into cannonballs and fired them at the cat, who was asleep in front of the fire. The first ball hit the cat squarely on the ear. She leapt up, caught her tail in the flames and screeched out of the room in search of a nice cool saucer of milk in which to soothe it. Still no reaction from his mum. So Jack crawled round to the back of the sofa and sprang, lion-like, onto her shoulders.

"Boo!" he shouted. This did get a reaction. Jack was removed from the sitting room by the seat of his pyjamas and dumped, unceremoniously, on the cold marble floor in the hall.

"When you have found a book, you may come back in," said his mum, and she disappeared back into the sitting room, shutting the door firmly behind her.

"Oh dear," said Jack, after a long pause. The only light in the hall came from the street lamp outside, which cast a deep red shadow over one wall. The shadow flickered as something flew in front of the light. Jack ducked down behind the telephone table and shut his eyes.

"Oh dear," he said again. "I don't like bats!" Jack had spent too much time hiding and too little time looking. They weren't bats at all, they were moths.

When he had summoned up enough courage Jack tiptoed to the bottom of the vast staircase. It spiralled upwards towards a large black hole at the top of the house. The white banisters stood out in the dark and, twisting as they did round and round in ever decreasing circles, they looked to Jack like a giant ribcage.

"I'm not scared," he whispered to himself. He didn't want to speak too loud in case the bogeyman heard him. Not that he believed in the bogeyman! Of course he didn't. It was just that if the bogeyman *did* exist and *was* hiding behind the bathroom door waiting to pounce, Jack didn't want to annoy him, because the biggest insult you can pay the bogeyman is to say you're not frightened of him. Frightening children half to death is his job, you see.

Jack started to climb the stairs. He took the first three steps very slowly, keeping his left hand in front of his eyes and feeling his way along the banister rail with his right.

Once he had reached the fourth step he was starting to feel more confident. This was easy. He was in his own house. His mother was downstairs. It was only going to take him a minute or so to reach his room and – *what was that noise?* He stopped dead. Something was groaning underneath the staircase. He took another step and froze with terror. There it was again. He couldn't be sure that it was definitely a groan. It could have been a rumbling sound. The sort his tummy made when he got home from school and was waiting for lunch. That was it. His worst nightmare. It was a hungry troll, burrowing up through the floorboards to make a meal out of him. He'd read about trolls. They liked the taste of little boys, especially when they were wearing pyjamas, and now there was one living under the stairs in his house!

He wanted to call out to his mum, but he knew she wouldn't hear him. There was only one thing to do. Run as fast as he could into his parents' bedroom and hope the troll wouldn't follow. He gritted his teeth, pulled up his pyjama bottoms so as not to trip over them, and set off up the last few steps to the landing.

The troll didn't make a sound to start with, until Jack stumbled on a loose floorboard. You should have heard the groan that it let out then. It made the hairs on the back of Jack's neck stick out like porcupine needles. He shot up the last few remaining steps like a rocket, dived into his parents' bedroom and slammed the door behind him.

The bedroom smelt familiar in that comforting way that all parents' bedrooms do. Jack sat with his back against the door and heaved a huge sigh of relief.

84

"Trolls!" he said to himself. "Honestly, Jack, what will you dream up next? Ghosts?" He laughed at his own stupidity. "Pull yourself together. That groaning noise was probably just squeaky floorboards!"

A cold wind blew gently across his face as he stood up to leave. He looked over to the far corner of the room where the wind had come from. Through the darkness he could just make out a swirling shape that was moving across the floor towards him.

"A ghost!" he squealed. He stood transfixed by this terrifying apparition. The shape was floating across the carpet, twisting and flapping like an enormous winged snake. He grabbed hold of the door handle and pulled it for all he was worth. It wouldn't open. He could feel the velvety wings of the serpent brushing against his back. He tugged at the handle again. This time the door opened and

Jack tumbled out of the room just as the wind dropped and the curtain fell back into its normal position in front of the open window.

Jack was a nervous wreck. The idea of his mum reading a bedtime story to him was becoming less and less attractive. He had one more flight of stairs to climb before he reached his own bedroom, and he had serious doubts about ever making it alive.

The bathroom stood between him and the foot of the stairs to the loft. The bathroom meant only one thing to Jack. The bogeyman. He knew exactly what the bogeyman looked like. He was very tall and fantastically gooey. So gooey, in fact, that he left a trail of slime behind him wherever he went. His hair was made out of green pond weed and he had lily pads instead of feet. What he actually did to children, Jack was not entirely sure, but he had a notion that he liked to slip into their clothes in the middle of the night, so that they were all wet and cold when they put them on in the morning.

Jack edged along the wall outside the bathroom, trying to be as quiet as he possibly could. He held his breath and ducked down as he passed the door, so that the bogeyman couldn't see him even if he was spying on Jack through the keyhole. Jack knew that the bogeyman was in there. He could hear that all too familiar dripping sound that kept him awake most nights and made him sleep with his head under his pillow. It was the slime dripping off the bogeyman's cape onto the linoleum floor.

Jack took his next breath when he reached the half landing on the way up to the loft. The worst was over. He had successfully escaped the grasp of the bogeyman

and all that stood now between him and the safety of his
bedroom was one short flight of stairs . . . and the fire
monster! The fire monster! How could he have forgotten
about the fire monster?!

The fire monster slept outside Jack's bedroom. For two
years it had been scratching at Jack's door in the middle
of the night begging to be let in, but Jack had never opened
the door. The monster pretended to be lonely, whimpering
pathetically about how cold it was outside on the landing,
and could it come in to warm itself in Jack's bed. But Jack
was wise to the monster's tricks. He knew that all it really
wanted to do was to roast him with its fiery breath until
he was as pink as a marshmallow.

Two red eyes stared at Jack over the top of the stair-

case. A dreadful smell of scorched fur surrounded the fire
monster's body as it lay sleepily on guard outside the bedroom door. Jack knew that he only had one chance. He
would have to fight the monster now, before it woke
up. He lunged forward and grasped its matted fur
with both hands. The monster twisted in his hands and
lashed out with its sharp claws. Jack rolled the monster
over onto its back and tried to pin its legs down, but the
monster was too quick for him. In a flash, the cat sprung
from Jack's clutches and ran off down the stairs, dragging
its scorched tail behind it.

Jack fell through his bedroom door, clambered onto
a box of bricks and switched the light on. He had made
it!

Thirty seconds later, Jack's mum heard the most peculiar noise. It sounded like a herd of elephants on roller skates charging downstairs. She barely had time to put her newspaper down before Jack flew into the room at a hundred miles an hour and buried his head in the pillows on the sofa.

"Did you get a book?" she said.

Jack kept his head hidden and waved his treasured prize in the air.

His mum took the book from him. "There. You see," she said. "That wasn't so hard, was it?"

Jack came out from under the pillows and snuggled up close to his mum.

"Now, what have you brought for me to read?"

Jack stuck his thumb in his mouth. He liked a good bedtime story and he was looking forward to this one.

"Dracula," said Jack. "It's my favourite."

The Litter Bug

In the olden days people never wore trousers. They all wore tights. The reason for this was quite simple. A rat cannot crawl up the inside of a pair of tights, but a trouser leg offers the greatest temptation known to rats, and in the olden days there were rats everywhere. So I ask you, if you had the choice between wearing tights or having a rat up your trousers, which would you choose?

Rats in those days used to be enormous. They would slip out of their ditches or sewers at night and stuff themselves silly on all the rubbish that people threw into the street. The more they ate, the bigger and fatter they became. Some were as big as dogs and roamed the streets in packs. If ever food became hard to find they would attack babies in their prams and chew off their fingers.

Then, one day, a clever man, called Mr Dustbin, realised that if he was ever to get rid of these ferocious rats, he would have to get rid of the rubbish first. So he invented a large bucket into which people could throw their rubbish. Then every Monday he would collect these large buckets and take the rubbish to a secret place where the rats couldn't find it.

The rats soon grew thin and hungry because they had nothing to eat, and in a very short time all the rats in the world died out. Mr Dustbin, however, grew rich and fat on all the money he made from collecting his buckets and retired to a very nice villa in Portugal, where he sat by a swimming pool for the rest of his life and drank beer.

All was well for a hundred years. Then Mr Dustbin died and with him died the memory of the rats. People had forgotten how awful it had been living with those vicious packs of slinky grey nibblers, and they slipped back into their old ways. Litter appeared on the streets again. Empty cans, greasy fish and chip wrappings, old newspapers and broken glass bottles once again lay in festering heaps by the side of the road.

The difference, though, was that this time there were no rats left to eat the rubbish. They had all died because of Mr Dustbin's cunning invention. So the piles of litter just grew bigger. In six weeks city centres throughout the land were overshadowed by vast amounts of plastic food cartons and scrunched up sweet papers. Waves of soggy cardboard boxes, mouldy food and rotting shoes sloshed out of the cities into the countryside, and it was not long before a National Emergency was announced. Great Britain was being buried under a top soil of stinking rubbish.

School children were given a shovel and a wheelbarrow and told to clean up the mess. Lessons were cancelled. Classes spent their days rushing to the seaside with wheelbarrows full of rotting waste and dumping the contents into

the sea. But it was all to no avail. The litter mountain kept on growing, and all because of one person.

Her name was Bunty Porker. She was as large as a double decker bus and to all who knew her, it was obvious why. She never stopped eating. Thirteen packets of cereal, five pounds of cheese, sixty-four slices of bread and a lorry load of chocolate buttons for breakfast. Eleven packets of crisps for elevenses, and another twelve for twelveses. Then lunch. This was when the serious eating of the day began for Bunty.

Aeroplanes from China flew in her first course. One thousand packets of rice, which she would boil up and serve with a knob of butter on top. This was followed by a vat of frozen peas, as many turkey burgers as she could eat in ten minutes (generally about two hundred), and a microwave full of chips. Pudding was simple. She went down to the local ice cream factory and ate it.

At four o'clock in the afternoon Bunty always felt peckish, so she would make herself some sandwiches. As many as would fit on the kitchen table was usually sufficient, but more often than not she would break into a crate of biscuits and devour those too.

Three hours later it was suppertime. Take-aways were her favourite. She would order twelve Indian curries, and ten Chinese set meals for six, then pop down to the local hamburger restaurant for a milkshake and twenty seven half-pounders with double helpings of everything. And once in bed, a cup of warm milk and a shortbread biscuit to aid digestion.

It was not the vast quantity of food which Bunty ate that was the problem. The litter mountain grew, because everything she ate was wrapped in plastic or came in a box, and she had to dispose of the wrappings somewhere.

She made herself a mega-large mackintosh with extra deep pockets. During the day she filled these pockets with her litter. Come nightfall, she slipped onto the streets and emptied her foul cargo into other people's front gardens, into duck ponds in the park, into bus shelters and shop doorways. Bunty was a litter lout of the most ginormous proportions.

It was not long before the litter mountain was as tall as two mountains. It stretched up through the clouds as far as the eye could see. On the ground its effect was devastating. Lakes disappeared, hills were flattened, cities came to a standstill as the streets clogged up. The country was quite literally a wasteland. People were trapped in their houses and animals buried underground. Bunty was the only person who ever went outside. She was the only person big enough to wade through swamps of old nappies and black banana skins. She was the only person who could stand the foul pong that hung over the land like a damp blanket.

Then the insects came. To them the pong was heaven. It was like waking up in the morning and smelling toast downstairs. The insects couldn't help themselves. One whiff of the litter mountain and they were drawn towards it. They came from all over the world. Fat flies from America, wolf spiders from Australia, mosquitoes from Africa and big black bugs, the size of fifty pence pieces, from Europe.

It was the Queen who first decided that enough was enough. She rang up the Prime Minister in the middle of the night.

"Yes?" said the Prime Minister sleepily as he sat up in bed.

"Queen here," said the Queen. "What are you going to do about the rubbish? I can't get out to walk the Corgis!"

"Your Majesty," said the Prime Minister, "I had no idea. I'll call a Cabinet meeting straight away and we'll draw up a plan of action."

"You do that," said the Queen, "but hurry. They're only little dogs and they can't hang on much longer."

"Of course," said the Prime Minister. "I'll do everything I can!"

The Cabinet decided that there was only one way to deal with the problem. Catch Bunty.

That night, the army was called in. Twenty thousand troops marched, or rather squelched, into London. The

Commanding Officer was a red faced man with a bristly moustache. His name was Colonel Buffy.

"Leave it all to me, Prime Minister!" he shouted. "My troops have been fully camouflaged – we've stuck bits of litter in our hats. This Bunty girly will never see us coming. We'll have her locked up within the hour."

Meanwhile, Bunty was not aware that any of this was happening. She was busy stuffing the pockets of her mega-large mackintosh with empty baked bean tins, ready for that night's litter drop.

Bunty left her house as the church clock was striking midnight. The moon was hidden behind a motionless cloud. She bellyflopped into the sticky black river that flowed outside her front door and swam down the road to the foot of the litter mountain. As she heaved herself out of the slime she heard a rustling behind her. She turned to look, but all she could see was litter. She carried on up the mountain. There it was again. That same noise. Only it wasn't just behind her now, it was all around. She peered again through the darkness to see what it was, and this time she definitely saw the rubbish moving. There was something underneath it, trying to push its way out.

"Over here, men," whispered Colonel Buffy. "There she is."

The Colonel pointed at the huge shadowy figure of Bunty standing on the rubbish heap. "You all know what to do. Form a circle round her, then close in and catch her."

"Erm . . . sir," said a weedy soldier, "don't you think she's a bit big for us, sir?"

"Nonsense," said the Colonel, "she's a little girly. No

95

problem." Then he barked, "Forward, men."

Bunty was watching the litter mountain for any further signs of movement. Everything had suddenly gone very quiet and still. The rustling had stopped.

"I must have imagined it," she said to herself. Then she turned and continued climbing.

Suddenly the air was filled with screaming and shouting. There were soldiers everywhere, carrying nets and waving sticks. Litter flew into the air as their heavy boots crashed down the slope towards her. More in terror than bravery, Bunty stood her ground. She was quickly surrounded and held tight by Colonel Buffy's men.

"Bunty Porker?" said the Colonel. "You're a litter bug. You're a menace. You're coming with me."

Bunty looked around at the camouflaged faces. Twenty thousand soldiers didn't seem that many to her. She turned back to the colonel.

"Well, actually," she said, "I'd rather not, if you don't mind."

Then she swung her massive arms around her head, until she looked a little bit like a helicopter, and flattened the lot of them.

"Of course," she said to herself, as she plodded on up the mountain, "those soldiers must have made that rustling sound, and the moving litter was them crawling towards me! How stupid of me to be scared. Well, at least I can dump my baked bean tins in peace now!"

But Bunty was wrong. The soldiers had been as quiet as mice. Something else had made the rustling sound. Something else had been burrowing away underneath the mountain trying to get out.

Do you remember the rats? The ones that grew into monster rats from eating all the rubbish. The ones that nibbled babies' fingers. They all died out, didn't they? But Bunty's litter mountain had attracted a different kind of visitor. Do you remember the big black bugs from Europe?

As Bunty reached the top of the mountain, she felt something shift under her feet. A long sharp wire pricked her ankle. She jumped backwards. It wasn't a wire. It couldn't be, it was twitching and it was pushing its way out through the side of the mountain. It looked exactly like a feeler on the top of a beetle's head, but that wasn't possible. It was over thirty feet long. No bug was that big ... Bunty's heart nearly stopped. "Unless the big black bugs from Europe have been eating all the rubbish, and have grown into giant bugs!" she screamed.

The mountainside opened up in front of her. Two enormous black pincers flashed past her head, four leathery wings beat the air and knocked her off her feet. Six hairy legs scuttled out of the hole.

Bunty sat there with her cheeks wobbling and her mouth open. The Litter Bug was hungry. With one enormous gloop, the giant bug sucked up three tons of litter and licked his lips. Bunty Porker didn't stand a chance. She disappeared along with all the rest of the rubbish.

The Litter Bugs soon ate all the litter and Bunty's mountain was reduced to a mere compost heap within a month. When the rubbish ran out, the Litter Bugs flew away in search of food elsewhere, but people had learnt their lesson. They never threw litter onto the street again. They always put it in a dustbin, as Mr Dustbin had taught them to, all those years before.

So if you ever drop litter, do watch out for the bugs.
They're never far behind you.

Goblin Mountain

Joseph Alexander lived in the shadow of an enormous mountain that towered over his parents' cottage. He had read many frightening stories about the mountain; about travellers who had climbed the craggy rockface never to be seen again; about the bands of fierce goblins that lived in the caves half way up and dined on the flesh of little children; about the giant eagle that ruled its rocky domain from a nest perched high up in the clouds.

Joseph treated the mountain with all the respect that these stories demanded. He never went near it. Yet in spite of his fear, he could not live so close to the mountain and not be fascinated by it. He would sit on the window ledge in his bedroom, for hours on end, reading and re-reading these gruesome tales.

He was not a naughty child, but he was thoughtless. Whenever he had finished a story he would tear the pages out of the book, open his window, throw the pages out, and watch them as they fluttered away across the garden towards the mountain. They looked so pretty, like large white butterflies. Joseph never once thought that what he was doing was wrong. Even when his father shouted at him for destroying something as precious as a book, he'd simply smile dreamily and say, "I thought I'd plant *new* books, Father, by scattering the pages across the mountainside."

The day arrived when there was not a single book left in the house. Joseph had torn them all up and thrown them out of the window. His mother was in tears. His father stormed around downstairs, banging doors.

"Now we have nothing to read, Joseph. Don't you see how wicked you have been?" wept his mother.

"Go upstairs to the attic," ordered his father. "You will remain locked in there until you have learnt to be sorry for what you have done!"

"What have I done?" said Joseph pathetically.

"You have only lost, forever, stories that have been treasured for generations!" shouted his father. "Now, upstairs!"

The attic was very dark. The only light came from a tiny window high up in the roof, but it had never been opened and a thick covering of dead leaves made a very effective curtain. Joseph shivered as he tried to make himself comfortable. It wasn't easy. The floor of the attic was covered in old nails and machine parts that his father had stored away, but had long since forgotten.

That night, Joseph couldn't sleep. It wasn't the eerie screeching of the barn owl that kept him awake, but his own thoughts. A book was just bits of paper stuck together with glue. It didn't matter that he had destroyed his parents' library. There were plenty of other books. They could buy some more. It didn't make sense to apologise.

He didn't see why he should. Mind you, he didn't want to spend another night in the attic. If he could just open that window, he'd be able to escape across the roof.

He scrabbled around in the half light and found a dusty old trunk buried in a corner. It was just the right height for him to reach the window latch. He took hold of one of the handles and gave it an almighty tug. It didn't move. It was much too heavy.

"There's probably a dead body inside," he joked with himself. Then he undid the lock and pushed the creaking lid open.

There was no dead body. In fact the trunk was empty, save for a large black book covered in cobwebs. He expected the book to be too heavy to lift, but when he took a firm grip of the cover he discovered that it was as light as a feather. So why had the trunk been so heavy?

The book was very old. On its cover it had a picture of a giant eagle perched on top of a mountain. Inside it was full of symbols and signs that meant nothing to Joseph. What he did recognise, however, were the pictures. Ugly faces, twisted bodies, evil eyes. The book was covered with pictures of goblins.

Joseph was hooked. He had never seen a book like it. Each page wove its magic around him and forced him to read on. There were pictures of goblins changing into frogs, of goblins floating in mid-air, of goblins summoning the devil from cracks in the mountain face. In almost no time at all Joseph had finished it, and even though he hadn't understood a single word, he was sure it was an ancient book of Magic Spells.

It was also the largest book he had ever read. Each

page was the size of a desk top.

You can guess what happened next. Driven by over-whelming temptation, Joseph tore every page out of its black leather binding. He dragged the empty trunk into position, climbed on top, and pushed the window till it opened, then he threw the pages out, one by one. Joseph was spell bound as they floated away across the garden, like a flock of beautiful white birds. But as the pages reached the mountain they burst into flame, and out of each flame sprung a black crow that flew up into the clouds and was lost from sight.

The spell was broken. Joseph was suddenly afraid. The cover of the book, which he was still holding, became hot, and the eyes of the giant eagle shone like two red coals in the darkness. With a scream he hurled the cover out of the window and watched it spiral downwards into the branches of his mother's favourite apple tree. The tree burst into flames and, in a second, was reduced to a black and charred stump. Sitting on top of the stump was a giant eagle.

Joseph's mother heard his scream and came running. She took the stairs to the attic three at a time. She heard Joseph scream for a second time as she fumbled with the key in the lock. The lock turned and she burst into the room, only to be knocked backwards by a fierce gust of wind. A giant eagle's feather settled on the floor next to her, and she looked up just in time to see her son's legs disappearing through the window. The eagle wheeled round towards the mountain. Clasped in its talons was the tiny, helpless, whimpering figure of Joseph Alexander.

The eagle seemed to lose interest in him as it circled

its nest. It just let go. Joseph fell like a stone. If it hadn't been for the trees stretching out their branches to catch him and let him down gently, he would surely have fallen to his death.

"Beware," said a whispering voice in Joseph's ear. "Beware!"

He spun round to see who it was, but there was no one there. A tree, bent over by the wind, brushed Joseph's shoulder.

"Beee . . . warre!" whispered the voice again. It was the tree talking.

"Beware of what?" said Joseph, but the wind had stopped blowing and the tree had straightened up. There was no reply.

Joseph looked around him. He had landed on a ledge by the entrance to a vast cave. He crawled inside and huddled up against the wall, for fear that the eagle might return for an early supper. The cave stank. It was the nauseating stench of rotten meat. Joseph wondered what type of beast could possibly live in such conditions.

"Goblins? Surely not," he said to himself. "They only exist in story books. They aren't real."

"Oh yes we are!" said a rasping voice nearby. The goblin pushed his warty nose into Joseph's face and grasped Joseph's neck with his webbed fingers. "And now . . . you're coming with me."

Joseph was dragged through a maze of dripping wet stone passages by a chain that the goblin had fastened round his neck. In the distance Joseph could hear voices chattering excitedly. As he approached them the passage opened out into a vast underground cavern. Black crows were perched all around the roof and sitting against the walls were row upon row of stinking goblins.

They leapt to their feet when he came in and jostled around him. Some poked him with sticks and pinched his legs, others simply came too close and breathed their foul breath all over him.

There were three loud knocks. A white haired goblin had entered the chamber through a door at the back. He had a goat skin cloak around his shoulders and carried a thorny cudgel in his hand.

"Let the trial commence!" he roared, and everyone took their seats again, leaving Joseph in the middle of the goblin court.

"You are accused, Joseph Alexander, of wilfully destroying the Great Book of Tharg, containing the mystical, ancient secrets of this magic mountain. Have you anything

to say before I pass sentence?"

"What about my trial?" shouted Joseph. "Aren't you going to listen to what I have to say in my defence?"

"No," said the judge. "That is not the goblin way."

A roar of approval came from the other goblins.

"Chop his head off," shouted one.

"Bury him in a vat of goose fat," screamed another.

"But I didn't mean to do it!" cried Joseph. "I promise I'll never do it again!"

"Too late!" declared the judge. "You have torn up too many books for me to believe you now. You're guilty!"

"No," shouted Joseph.

"Take him away and plant him with the others."

A ripple of laughter went around the court.

"What do you mean, plant me?" said Joseph, as a hundred goblin fingers lifted him up.

"You are to be turned into a tree," said the judge. "Just like all the other children who think it is acceptable behaviour to tear up their books! Trees make paper. Paper makes books! One day you will be chopped down to make paper. One day you will be stuck together to make a book. One day you will be torn to shreds by some other miserable child!"

There was a loud cheer. The white haired goblin left the court and Joseph was carried out onto the mountainside by the mob.

They dug a deep hole and threw Joseph into it. He looked around despairingly at all the other trees, but they were powerless to help. Then he heard a familiar voice.

"I warned you to beware," whispered the tree in his ear. It was one of the other children who had been planted alongside him.

"But I didn't know!" Joseph cried. "I didn't know . . . I didn't know . . ."

"You didn't know what?" said his mother who had finally managed to open the door to the attic.

"What?" said Joseph, who didn't know where he was.

"You've been screaming your head off for the last ten minutes," she said.

Joseph was still in the attic. The black crows, the giant eagle, the goblin court, it must have all been a dream.

Joseph threw his arms round his mother.

"I promise I'll never tear up another book in my whole life," he wept. "I don't want to be a tree!"

"I'm sure you don't," said his mother as she hugged him back. "Come on. It's time you went to bed." Then she picked Joseph up and carried him downstairs.

In the attic an icy wind gusted in through the open window, picked up the giant eagle's feather and blew it out across the garden towards the mountain.

Sweets

You only have to go into a shop and you can see them. Horrible children, tugging at their mothers' dresses, or running round the display counters screaming their heads off and blasting imaginary spacemen. Red-cheeked cherubs looking innocently out from behind a rack of clothes, where they have just spat in the pockets of all the trousers. Dirty fingers in the food hall. Grubby noses smeared across squeaky-clean plate glass windows. And worst of all, those high pitched voices, whining and wingeing.

"I want some sweets!" That oh-so familiar cry that stretches your nerves to breaking point and turns normally placid adults into gibbering wrecks.

"I'm bored! I want a present. I want a toy or some sweets. Why can't I have some sweets? I want to buy something. Can I have a pony or some sweets or an electric tractor? It's not fair, you never buy me anything!" Moan moan, sob sob, whimper whimper, bellyache.

Thomas Ratchet was a horrible child. When his mother took him shopping he would misbehave so badly that people would stare and tut tut under their breath.

One day he was particularly naughty. His mother had taken him and his little sister Emily to the local supermarket to do the week's shopping.

"Is this your child?" said the store detective to Mrs Ratchet. She was trying to pack her groceries at the checkout.

"Oh dear. What has he done now?" said Mrs Ratchet.

"He was eating the bananas," said the store detective.

"I was bored," said Thomas.

"Not only that, I caught him using a trolley as a racing car."

"Oh," she said. Thomas didn't look at all ashamed. He looked rather pleased with himself.

"Can I have some sweets now, Mum?"

"Then," continued the detective, "he emptied a carton of yoghurt on the floor to see how far he could slide on it. He stole some chocolate out of an old lady's basket, he changed over the price labels on the cereal packets, he climbed onto the top shelf of the biscuit section shouting, 'look at me I'm a monkey' and, finally, he poured a pint of cream down the front of my trousers when I tried to stop him."

Thomas laughed. He'd had a great time. In fact he hadn't had so much fun since he switched off that chest freezer in Sainsbury's and turned the delicatessen counter into an ice cold swimming pool.

The store detective frog-marched Thomas out of the shop. One hand on the seat of his trousers, the other firmly grasping his right ear. Mrs Ratchet hurried along behind, muttering, "Sorry" and "I don't know what's come over him. He's not normally this naughty." But, of course, he was.

"Can I have some sweets *now*?" said Thomas, when they were standing on the pavement.

"No you cannot," replied his mother.

They visited the chemist next to buy some nappies for Emily.

"Stay right next to me, Thomas," said his mother, who was starting to sound annoyed. "And don't touch anything."

To Thomas, this was like saying: "Run away and lay your hands on anything you can find. If you can break it, so much the better." He always did the opposite to what he was told.

In the chemist's shop he fired toothpaste at a small dog, he fed lollipops to a baby, without removing the wrapper, and he used a bottle of suntan lotion to write his name all over the floor.

"Get him out of here," shouted the manageress, "and don't come back!"

"Can I have some sweets first, Mum?" whined Thomas.

Poor Mrs Ratchet was in a right old tizz as she was bundled out of the shop.

"Sorry," she muttered for the second time that morning. "I really don't know what's come over him. He's not normally this naughty." But of course, he was.

"Now just behave yourself, Thomas," said his mother.

"I will if I can have some sweets," he moaned.

In the newsagent's he demanded a comic, in the butcher's he broke a dozen eggs when he used them to play catch, in the baker's he glued up the charity box by cramming a jam doughnut into the slot, and in the bank he tripped up an old man, by trying to crawl through his legs.

"Walk properly, Thomas," his mother said wearily as they left the bank and started for home. "Do try to keep up."

"I can't," he said, "I want some sweets." Then, "You *never* buy me any sweets!"

"If you behaved yourself for once," she replied, "then I might."

"I want sweets!" Thomas shouted again. "You're horrible. I never want to see you again!" With that he took to his heels and ran off round the corner.

He could hear his mother's voice calling after him. "Thomas! Come back here!" Her voice got further and further away, until, finally, he couldn't hear it at all. Then he stopped running.

He looked around to see where he was. He had run into a narrow alleyway. The buildings were tall and thin and the pavement was made of cobblestones. All of the windows were shuttered, and short flights of worn stone steps led up to heavy wooden doors. The street looked deserted. Thomas was just about to turn around and go back the way he had come, when he heard a squeaking sound above his head. He looked up sharply, half expecting to see a bat or something, but all he could see was an old shop sign, creaking gently in the wind.

The sign said quite simply:

SWEETS. *Bang Three Times on Door and Wait.*

Thomas didn't need to be told twice. He banged three times on the door. Nobody came. He waited for a minute

or so and banged again. Harder this time and longer. He was making enough noise to wake the dead, when he heard footsteps approaching. They shuffled towards him and stopped on the other side of the door. Thomas heard a jangle of keys, then a bolt being pulled back. The door edged open and he found himself looking straight into the bloodshot eyes of a tiny rickety old man, with wispy white hair and rotten teeth.

"The sign says bang *three* times," he hissed.

"I wanted some sweets," said Thomas, "and you were taking too long."

"Sometimes," said the old man, "it doesn't pay to be hasty. You must be Thomas Ratchet."

"How did you know that?" said Thomas, following the old man inside.

"I've been expecting you for quite some time," said the old man, as he shut the front door behind Thomas and slid the heavy bolt home.

The old man's shop didn't look anything like a sweet shop. It was dark and damp and smelled of cats. Long yellow strips of sticky paper hung from the ceiling, covered with thousands of dead flies. Mice ran in and out of the furniture. In the corner Thomas thought he could see a large pile of bodies, but when his eyes got used to the light, he realised that it was only a pile of shop window dummies.

"I thought those were bodies!" he said to the old man.

"Don't be ridiculous. This is a sweet shop. Now, what would you like?"

"Lemon sherberts, liquorice twisters and six sticks of rock!" said Thomas.

"Your favourites," said the old man.

"You seem to know a lot about me."

"I also know that when you go shopping with your mother, you are the worst behaved boy in the world," said the old man, retreating into a second room behind the counter.

"I'm not," said Thomas. "If she bought me sweets I'd be as good as gold. Are you sure those are shop window dummies in the corner?"

"Why do you ask?" said the old man reaching for a large net hanging on the back of the door.

"I thought I saw their eyes move," said Thomas.

The old man laughed as he unhooked the net and flicked a switch on the wall. Thomas heard an engine start up in the next room.

"So where are my sweets?" he said.

"Through here," said the old man, beckoning Thomas through into the back room. "You don't like shops, then?"

"I hate them," said Thomas. "They're so boring. There's never anything to do."

"What a pity," said the old man. "Still, I expect you'll get used to them."

Thomas was about to ask what he meant by that last remark, when the old man suddenly scooped him up in his net and deposited him into a vast cauldron of churning, white, papier maché.

When Thomas woke up he felt very stiff.

"This old man is a trickster," he thought to himself. "He hasn't got any sweets. I'm getting out of here right now!"

He tried to move his leg, but it must have been

trapped, because it wouldn't move.

"He's tied me up!" thought Thomas. "I'll bash him for this."

He tried to move his arm, but that too was stuck fast. As were his head and feet and hands! He was trapped! He could just move his eyes, and looking down he suddenly realised what had happened. It was too horrible for words! The old man had set him in papier maché.

"I don't want to be a shop dummy!" shouted Thomas. But he was.

Thomas spends all his time in shops nowadays. He stands in the window and watches the world pass by.

If you look closely at shop dummies in future you might see Thomas. His eyes will follow you down the street, but it won't be you that he's interested in. He's waiting for his mother to find him. She stopped at his window last week and looked straight at him. She seemed to recognise Thomas's face, but she obviously couldn't remember where from.

When she does remember, I think she'll come and get him, don't you?

The Top Hat

When Benjamin was born everyone thought he looked like a baby rabbit.

"I say," said Benjamin's father, "I've just had a whizzo idea. Let's nickname the little chap Benjamin Bunny!"

This suggestion was greeted with much hearty laughter, and from that day forward Benjamin had to suffer the embarrassment of being called Bunny Rabbit in public.

His favourite uncle bought him a shiny black top hat for his first birthday present. Nobody could understand why.

"Oh really," said Uncle Jonathan, "has nobody ever heard of a magician's top hat?"

"Well of course we have," screeched Benjamin's mother.

"So what does a magician keep in his hat?"

"His head?" chipped in Benjamin's father. Then he realised what a stupid thing that was to say, so he shut up.

"A RABBIT!" said Uncle Jonathan. "I thought that was obvious. Benjamin's nickname is rabbit. Rabbits live in top hats. So I've given him a top hat."

"Oh," said Benjamin's mother. Then she added, "Yes. Well, it's a super present, anyway. Thank you, Jonathan. I'll put it in a cupboard until Bunny Rabbit is old enough to wear it."

Benjamin, however, had other ideas. The next day he found the cupboard where his mother had hidden the top hat. He climbed onto a chair, crawled across her newly ironed blouses and dug it out of her socks at the back of the shelf. When his mother found him, Benjamin was standing in the middle of a crumpled heap of her clothes, with the top hat sitting squarely on his shoulders. His head had completely disappeared up inside it.

From that day forward Benjamin and the top hat could not be separated. They became the best of friends and played together all day long. With the top hat to help him Benjamin could pretend to be anything from a circus ringmaster to a rich toff at the opera, from a coachman to the Prince of Wales, from a policeman to a scruffy young pickpocket. He used it as a handy storage jar for his marbles; as a frisbee, although it was an awful flier in strong winds; as a deep sea diver's boot, and even as a fishing net for catching tadpoles. There was nothing his top hat could not be, or do.

And yet all was not right. The hat started to take over Benjamin's life.

Benjamin woke up one morning and decided, quite suddenly, that everything in his room should look like a black top hat. He had a top hat lampshade, a top hat clock, a top hat bed and even a top hat bath, which was specially made for him by a firm of bespoke plumbers in

Saville Row. (So unique was the order, in fact, that they presented him with a free top hat toilet as well.)

He went around the house with a tin of black paint and sloshed it over anything that looked remotely like a top hat – his mother's saucepans, the waste paper baskets, the cat (that was a mistake), his wellington boots, all the flowerpots and his father's golf club bag.

Benjamin's parents became a little concerned. They tried to take his top hat away from him, but Benjamin made it absolutely clear that he could not live without it. He sat in the corner of the sitting room with a lampshade on his head and refused to eat anything until he got his top hat back. It took three days, but his parents returned it.

Fortunately for them, however, Uncle Jonathan's top hat only lasted for five years. Benjamin had worn it every day since his first birthday, when, one day, while he was diving off the springboard at the local baths, it simply fell apart. It disintegrated as he hit the water and floated away from him like wreckage from a sunken ship. Then, piece by soggy piece, it sank to the bottom of the pool.

Benjamin cried for a week. When he was told that he would have to wait until his next birthday before getting a new one, he locked himself in his room and cried for *ten* weeks non-stop. He came out on the morning of his sixth birthday.

"Well?" he said. "Where is it?"

Benjamin looked at his mother. His mother looked nervously at his father. His father coughed, smiled and looked straight back at his mother. Benjamin's mother looked at him. He was still looking at his mother. His mother looked away.

"Is something the matter?" said Benjamin.

"Bunny Rabbit," said his mother. Benjamin mistrusted her smile. "We haven't been able to find you a new top hat."

"They don't make them in your size any more," added his father hurriedly.

There was silence as they waited for Benjamin's reaction.

His ears went red first, then the tip of his nose. His eyebrows started to twitch independently of each other. His bottom lip quivered and jutted out so far that his jaw nearly cracked. A tiny little voice squeaked in the back of his throat. "But I wanted one!"

Tears streamed down his face as he stamped his foot, turned on his heels and stormed out of the room.

His mother ran after him. "We've organised a lovely party for you instead, Bunny. With a conjuror. He's supposed to be very good. We did try to buy you a top hat, but . . ."

She gave up. Benjamin was not listening. He had turned his back on his mother and was climbing the stairs. Half way up, he stopped. Then, without turning round, he uttered those four ugly words that all parents fear the most. "I really hate you," he said. Then he went back into his room and locked the door.

At half past three the doorbell rang and Benjamin's mother let the first of the party guests in. Ten minutes later the sitting room was full of little girls wearing pretty white party dresses, and thumping great boys with squeaky clean fingernails and well-scrubbed necks. They were sitting in a circle on the floor, in silence.

"I'll just see if Benjamin's ready yet," said his mother cheerfully as she handed out several more packets of crisps, tripped over a tiny boy called Martin, laughed nervously, and left the room.

Upstairs, Benjamin's father was trying to take the lock off Benjamin's bedroom door.

"It's no good," he said to his wife, "I can't open it." Then he put his mouth to the keyhole and said in his sternest voice, "If you don't come out now, Benjamin, I shall break this door down and carry you downstairs over my shoulder!" To his surprise he heard the key turn in the lock. The door opened and there stood Benjamin, dressed and ready for the party.

"Splendid!" said his mother. "Now we can all have fun!"

Benjamin smiled, but it wasn't a friendly smile, and the look in his eyes wasn't a friendly look. Something naughty was going on in his head, and his parents didn't know what.

"Hello, everyone," shouted Benjamin, as he ran into the sitting room. "Sorry I'm late, but I've just been feeding my pet spiders and they've all escaped!" The children screamed and leapt off the floor onto the furniture.

"They like to hide down the back of the sofa," he continued, "so if you see one give us a shout." The children screamed again, and leapt off the furniture back onto the floor.

Benjamin's mother laughed loudly. "Very funny, Bunny," she said, "but you don't keep pet spiders."

"No mother," replied Benjamin. The other children stopped crying and started to giggle at their own stupidity. "I keep long pink slimy worms instead!"

The scream was deafening as twelve children leapt back onto the sofa. It wobbled, then toppled over backwards and crushed Benjamin's father's toe as it landed.

"Who's got me a present?" demanded Benjamin, standing over the untidy heap of arms and legs.

"Me!" came a voice from the bottom.

"And me!" shouted several others.

"Well, aren't you going to give them to me, then?" he said.

The children disentangled themselves and clambered over each other to thrust their presents into Benjamin's arms. They waited expectantly as he tore open the wrapping paper. One by one the excitement on their faces turned to sadness as Benjamin threw their gifts over his shoulder into the wastepaper bin.

"These presents are useless," he announced bitterly. "Nobody's bought me a top hat. Thanks for absolutely nothing!" Then he went next door into the dining room.

Half the children wanted to cry. The other half wanted to go home.

"He doesn't mean it!" said Benjamin's mother, putting her arms around tiny Martin, who had spent all his pocket money buying Benjamin a Macho Man ground to air missile system. "Let's go next door for tea." Benjamin's father, who was sitting on the floor with a sock in one hand and his injured toe in the other, agreed.

The doorbell rang as they sat down at the table. Benjamin's father hobbled to the door and answered it.

"Good afternoon, sir," said a man in a long red cape and pointy black hat. "Marvin the Marvellous Magician at your service." The Magician bowed low, scraping his long white beard along the doorstep.

"Thank Heavens you've arrived," said Benjamin's father and he opened the door wide to allow Marvin the Marvellous Magician to bring his Box of Magic Tricks into the house.

"I hope you don't mind, good sir," said Marvin as he stood in the hall, "but I have taken the liberty of bringing along my assistant today. Perhaps I might be permitted to offer him sanctuary within your hallowed walls?"

Benjamin's father looked blankly at the Magician.

"Oh, of course," said Benjamin's father. "By all means."

Back in the dining room, Benjamin's mother was lighting the candles on the birthday cake. It was a large black top hat. The children had all perked up at the sight of it, and they joined in with a spirited chorus of Happy Birthday. Benjamin sat unmoved at the head of the table, cramming the last of the sausages into his mouth, cocktail sticks and all. When they had finished singing he blew out the candles and sat back in his chair.

"Did you make a wish, Bunny?" said his mother.

"Yes," said Benjamin. "I wished that this cake was a real top hat, not a boring old chocolate one."

"Well wishes sometimes come true," she said.

"Not this one," replied Benjamin, picking up the cake and squashing it down on top of tiny Martin's head. Martin started to cry again as chocolate ran down his forehead and dripped off the end of his nose. "Otherwise it wouldn't have squidged like that, would it?"

Benjamin's father's sock suddenly appeared round the edge of the door on the end of Benjamin's father's hand.

"It's show time!" said the sock. "Take your seats for Marvin the Marvellous Magician!"

Benjamin had decided that the best way to punish his parents for not buying him a new top hat was to not watch the magic show. So he screwed his eyes tightly shut and missed the Indian Rope Trick, some clever shuffling of a pack of cards and a trick where tiny Martin had a rubber egg broken over his head. Martin thought it was a real egg and left the room in tears for the third time. He spent the rest of the party trying to phone his mother to tell her to come and pick him up. However when Marvin the Marvellous Magician asked for the assistance of the Birthday boy, Benjamin reluctantly had to open his eyes and go and stand up in front of all his friends.

"Have you ever seen a person magicked out of thin air, young man?" said the Magician.

"Yes," replied Benjamin, trying to spoil it for the others.

"Ha ha! What a wag!" said Marvellous Marvin, crossly. "Now watch this empty box. I want you to say the magic words with me and before your very eyes, boys and girls, I shall make my assistant appear in this box, where previously he has not been."

Benjamin yawned.

"Iggly wiggly, curly piggly," he muttered, making himself sound as bored as he possibly could. Nothing happened for a second, then suddenly there was a flash of light inside the box. As the smoke cleared the shape of a small boy, about Benjamin's height, could clearly be seen crouching inside the box. There was a gasp of amazement as the boy stepped out and everyone broke into wild applause. Everyone, that is, except Benjamin. He was standing with his mouth wide open gazing at the top of the boy's head. You can imagine what he saw there, can't you? A shiny black top hat, and

it was just the right size.

The boy had a pale white face, and a permanently sad expression that made him look older than his six years. He was dressed like his father in a red cape, but he was also wearing a silver waistcoat embroidered with stars that glinted underneath the lights. Benjamin saw none of this. His attention was wholly fixed on the top hat. He had to have it, whatever the cost.

"Seeing as how you helped me most magnificently with that last trick," said Marvellous Marvin, interrupting Benjamin's thoughts, "and being as you are the Birthday Boy, you may have any prize you wish."

"I'd like his hat, please," said Benjamin without hesitation.

The boy assistant looked nervously at his father.

"Ah no. Sadly not the hat. Anything but that top hat," replied Marvellous Marvin, quickly. "It has been in my family for hundreds of years and contains all our magic. If we parted with that hat we would no longer be magicians. Choose again, young Benjamin."

The room had gone quiet. Benjamin took a step forward. "I must have that top hat," he said.

"And my father said no!" The pale faced boy spoke for the first time. "You have not been taught how to control its magic. It would be too dangerous."

Benjamin flashed a glance at his parents who were standing at the back of the room. He had a free run to the door if he chose to ... Yes! He darted forward and seized the top hat off the boy's head. The hat twisted in his hand, as if alive, and fell from his grasp. It wriggled across the carpet towards the magic box, but Benjamin was too quick for it. He snatched it up, tucked it under his arm, bolted upstairs to his bedroom, and locked the door. Marvellous Marvin and his son had not even moved.

Benjamin sat on his bed and stroked the top hat. He remembered blowing out the candles on his cake and thought, "Perhaps wishes do come true after all. This is the most beautiful top hat I have ever seen." Then he went over to the mirror and raised the hat above his head . . .

There was a furious banging on the door. It was the Magician and his son. "Don't put the hat on," they were shouting. "Whatever you do, don't put the hat on your head!" But they were too late.

The top hat was a perfect fit. It sat like a magnificent black pillar on the top of Benjamin's head. Then, as he was admiring it in the mirror, something very strange happened. The hat moved, just as it had done when Benjamin had stolen it from the boy downstairs. It wiggled and squirmed on his head, as if an animal were trapped inside. He took the hat off and turned it over. A large white rabbit hopped out. It bounded across the bedroom floor and hid underneath the bed. Benjamin looked inside the hat for a secret panel or a false bottom, but the hat was solid. He put it back on his head, and almost immediately it jiggled again.

The cries from the landing were becoming more insistent. Benjamin's parents had joined the Magician and his son.

"Throw the hat out of the window, Bunny," shouted his mother, anxiously.

"Push it under the door," added his father. Everyone glowered at him. Top hats do not naturally slide underneath doors.

Benjamin had discovered that if he wished for something hard enough while he was wearing the hat, it would appear seconds later from inside the hat.

"I wish I had a ten speed racing bike," he thought, holding the top hat tightly over his ears. A cold metal bar dug into the back of his neck, an oily chain stuck to his hair and Benjamin only just got the hat off in time before a silver bicycle popped out onto the floor.

On the landing Marvellous Marvin was trying to batter down the bedroom door with his shoulder.

"Do mind the paintwork," pleaded Benjamin's father.

"My good sir," said the Magician, haughtily, "if we don't get this door open in the next sixty seconds and get that hat off your son's head, I will not be held responsible for the consequences!"

"Oh," said Benjamin's father. "I see. Well, what are we waiting for?" And he launched a massive kick at the door with his good right foot and bruised his other toe.

In the bedroom, Benjamin was getting greedy. The mountain of toys was growing. Amongst other things, he had wished for two dogs, a pony, an electric car, a paddling pool full of lemonade, a Wendy House, a motorboat and sixty-five top hats. There was no room left to move.

As he put the top hat on again and wondered what to wish for next, the door burst open and Marvin the Marvellous Magician, his son with the pale face and Benjamin's parents tumbled into the room. They all looked furious.

Benjamin was suddenly afraid.

"I wish I wasn't here," he said, and then he realised what he had done. The magic top hat was still on his

head. There was a terrible rumbling from deep inside the hat's silk lining. Then a ripping and tearing as something fought to get out. There was a blast of hot air, the hat flew off Benjamin's head and a giant hand, with five enormous fingers, burst out into the room.

The Magician's son shouted to Benjamin, "I warned you not to meddle with powers you don't understand," but Benjamin did not hear him. The hand had swooped down, picked him up by the scruff of his neck and scuttled back into the shiny black top hat.

Benjamin never reappeared. Marvin the Marvellous Magician tried to conjure up the hand again, but he had no luck. Benjamin had been too greedy, and had used up all the hat's magic powers.

It's a sad fact, but nowadays, the only thing that

ever comes out of that particular magician's top hat is a teeny tiny voice that sounds just like Benjamin trying to say sorry.

The Childhood Snatcher

Amos Stirling was not very bright. He never had been. All through his life he had dreamt of being a great scientist. Not because he wanted to invent something useful to help others, but because he wanted to be famous. It was that simple. He wanted people to notice him when he walked down the street and say, "That's Amos Stirling. He's so intelligent. I wish I was as clever as him." But only a stupid man would wish for that, and Amos Stirling *was* a stupid man.

On the morning of his fortieth birthday Amos looked in the mirror and sighed deeply.

"I'm never going to be rich and famous," he admitted to himself. "What I need is a child who is a genius. People admire a clever child, and if they admire my child then they will admire me too."

So Amos Stirling advertised for a wife.

A timid woman from a tiny island off the north coast of Scotland read the advertisement. Her name was Betty and she too was forty years old. Betty was not fussy about who she married, just so long as she had a husband. Amos was a poor choice, but he would have to do.

Shortly after the wedding, Betty gave birth to a beautiful baby girl. Amos christened his daughter Albert.

"But Albert's a boy's name," wept Betty, when he first told her.

Amos puffed out his chest and made his voice sound important. "If the name Albert is good enough for Albert Einstein, the greatest scientist this world has ever known, then it's good enough for my daughter," he said, pompously.

"But Albert Einstein was a man," repeated Betty, who feared that her neighbours would laugh at her if she called her daughter Albert. Amos was not listening. He was dreaming of the day when his daughter would accept an award for being the most brilliant person on the planet. And he would be standing on the platform, right next to her.

The day that Betty and Albert came home from the hospital, Amos was busy transforming her room from a pretty pink playroom, into a cold white laboratory full of science books and computers.

"Don't you think there should be some toys in the room?" asked Betty.

"Toys!" laughed Amos. "What does Albert want with toys?" He leaned over her cot. "You want to be a genius, don't you my lovely? And we'll start tomorrow with a few simple sums."

"The child is only four days old, Amos," said Betty, as Amos left the room to plug in an electric calculator.

"That's why we're going to start with *simple* sums, my dear. I don't expect her to grasp the difficult ones for weeks yet."

As the weeks wore on, Betty saw less and less of her precious daughter. Amos spent ten hours a day in Albert's room. Some days he came out looking happy, but on other days his face was as black as thunder.

"She doesn't understand long division!" he ranted. "The girl is an idiot. Every time I ask her a question she gives me the same answer – Ga ga goo goo."

"She's a baby," said Betty. "That's how babies are meant to talk. If they didn't, they'd be grown ups."

"And do you know what else she did?" said Amos, completely ignoring his wife. "I was in the middle of explaining a most complicated algebraic equation when a robin landed on the window ledge. Albert stopped listening to me and looked at the robin instead. Then she started giggling. In the middle of a lesson! It's intolerable!"

The next day Amos cancelled his class with Albert, and used his free time to fit steel shutters onto the windows in her room. Robins could not be allowed to interfere with his daughter's education. From then on classes were conducted behind closed doors. Nobody could see in and Albert couldn't see out. Even Betty was forbidden to make a noise in the house during the daytime for fear that Albert might be distracted.

At nightime, however, the shutters were flung back and the windows opened wide to let in as much fresh air as possible. It was Amos's theory that fresh air increased the size of Albert's brain.

One night, at the stroke of midnight (Albert knew it

was midnight, because she had counted the chimes of the
grandfather clock), Albert was wakened by a strange noise
at the foot of her cot. It was a thump. A thump of boots, as
if someone had just flown in through her window. She was
too young to sit up, but she could hear shallow breathing,
and see a long shadow creeping towards her across the
ceiling. She started to cry, but a wrinkled hand, smelling of
chalk, covered her mouth, and a gentle old voice whispered
soothing words to calm her.

Albert's visitor was dressed in a long black cape. It
had a large hood which concealed most of his face. Only
the tip of his sharp, pink nose was visible. Over his back
he carried a black silk sack, which he slid over his head
and placed carefully on top of Albert's blanket.

"Good evening, Albert," he said. "I've been sent by

your father, Amos. They call me the Childhood Snatcher and we're going to be seeing a lot more of each other over the next few years."

Albert smiled at his kindly voice.

"Now, I need a hair," he continued. "A soft new hair from the top of your head." Then he leant forward, plucked one out and dropped it into his sack.

Albert never cried once. She just lay there and grinned, even when the childhood snatcher swirled his cape around his shoulders and disappeared through the window in a cloud of dust.

The next morning a strange transformation had taken place. When Betty came in to get Albert up, Albert turned away and wouldn't let her mother pick her up. She only wanted her father. This behaviour continued for several days until Betty could take no more. She burst into tears at the breakfast table.

"Albert doesn't love me any more," she cried.

"No," said Amos, cruelly. "She doesn't, does she? She still likes me, though, which is the main thing."

Poor Albert. There is nothing more precious to a child than its love for its mother and the Childhood Snatcher had stolen Albert's love away.

Meanwhile Amos was continuing with her lessons. When Albert should have been in the park feeding the ducks, he had her nose buried in a Chemistry text book. When she should have been crawling around on a rug playing with other children, he had her drawing complicated pictures of motor car engines. When she should have been sleeping, he raised his voice and shouted his facts and figures at her to keep her awake.

At six months old she still couldn't speak, but she had a fairly strong grasp of Quantum Physics.

The night before her first birthday, Albert received a second visit. She laughed and clapped as the Childhood Snatcher flew in through the open window.

"You liked that?" said the hidden face.

"Very much," said Albert, who was now talking. "Will you do it again? Flying is such fun!"

He interrupted her. "Your father wants to know if you're enjoying your lessons with him?" he said.

"Quite frankly, no," replied Albert. "It's all a bit boring, and *so* serious. When I feel happy I want to laugh, but Daddy doesn't let me."

The figure in black said nothing. Then suddenly he reached forward and plucked a second hair from Albert's head.

"I'll see you in one year's time," he said, and he flew back out of the window. Only this time Albert did not laugh and clap. Seeing the Childhood Snatcher fly was no longer funny to her.

In class the following day Albert asked her father who the Childhood Snatcher was.

"I've no idea," replied Amos. "I've never heard of him."

"But he said that you had sent him."

"Did he?" said Amos who was a little puzzled. "Well if he says I did, I must have done, but I wasn't aware of doing it."

Over the following months Albert grew as fast as any baby girl of eighteen months should do. Her mind, however, grew much faster. She knew things that only twenty-year-olds should know. She could not only speak fluent

English, but French, German and Spanish as well. She could do sums in her head that would take a computer five minutes to work out. And she had made her first investment on the Stock Market. Amos was delighted. It didn't matter to him that his daughter never laughed or smiled any more. She was a child genius and it was only a matter of time before the world's press started knocking on their door.

Betty tried hard to bring Albert up as a normal child. She often invited other boys and girls of Albert's age round to tea, and took them all down to the Adventure Playground to play on the swings. But Amos didn't like the distraction, and Albert found her friends, who were all still in nappies, painfully childish. It wasn't as if they could help her to learn faster. In fact they positively held her back.

The Childhood Snatcher reappeared on the eve of Albert's second birthday. He stood at the end of the bed and waited for her to wake up, but Albert was far too tired. Amos worked her so hard during the day that nothing could wake her at night. If Father Christmas had slid down the chimney and ho-ho'ed in her ear, she would still have slept on. So the Childhood Snatcher helped himself to a third hair from her head and flew away into the night.

When Albert awoke she was two. She went down to breakfast wearing her frumpiest dress and said to Betty, "Mother. If you want to give me a present for my birthday, don't ever invite my friends round to tea again. I am weary of them. They bore me with their silly talk."

Then she turned to Amos. "Father!" she shouted. "We

should have started my Greek lesson two minutes ago!"

Betty rose from the kitchen table and stood in front of Albert as she tried to leave the room.

"Mother, I haven't time for your games! It will only end in tears!" said Albert.

"Albert," said Betty, "you're turning into a boring, middle-aged woman and you're only two years old! You should be outside running around in the garden, getting grass stains on your pinafore, putting snails down your vest, breaking windows with a tennis ball. Not sitting upstairs all day, poring over dusty text books! You're getting old before you've had a chance to be young!"

There was a short silence. Amos folded his newspaper.

"I think you need to see a doctor, Betty," he said. "Besides, Albert doesn't need friends. She's got me!" Then he took Albert's arm and whisked her upstairs to the classroom.

Betty sat down at the kitchen table and wept for Albert's lost childhood.

The Childhood Snatcher had done his work. Albert had shunned her mother, she had stopped laughing and she had discarded her friends. For what? At the age of two years and one month she was offered a place at Oxford University to study anything she wanted. She passed her exams within three months and left Oxford to become personal advisor to the Prime Minister. All of this before her third birthday.

Amos had everything he had ever dreamt of. If Albert was on the television or had her picture taken by a newspaper, he was there, standing proudly by her side, with a smug look on his face that said, "This is *my* daughter, and *I* have made her what she is today. Aren't *I* clever?"

Albert went to bed at 9 o'clock on the night before she was three. She had finished the Chancellor's Budget speech during supper. As she lay awake reading the Oxford Dictionary, she heard a familiar noise on the window ledge. She looked up. The Childhood Snatcher floated into the room, his black cape billowing behind him.

"Good evening, Albert," he said, in his soft voice.

"I didn't expect to see you," she replied. "Has father sent you again?"

"Not this time," said the voice inside the black hood. "Tonight is the last time you will ever see me. Tonight I have come to finish my work."

"I thought it *was* finished," replied Albert. "As you can see, I no longer think like a child. What else is there for you to take from me?"

The Childhood Snatcher pushed the hood back off his face. He was old and wrinkled. His eyes sagged and his lips were blue.

"Your beauty," he said. "I cannot steal your childhood from you without removing the most important part – the way you look."

"You mean, you're going to make me look as if I was twenty-five?" asked Albert.

The Childhood Snatcher threw back his wizened face and laughed. He had no teeth.

"Albert," he said finally. "Twenty-five is still a child, ninety-five is old!"

Then he leant forward and plucked a fourth hair from the top of her pretty little head.

Albert screamed. Her parents rushed into her room, but they were too late. The Childhood Snatcher had gone

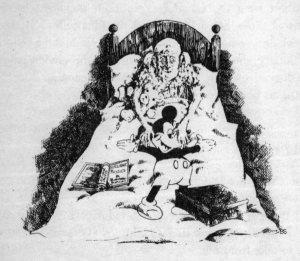

and, sitting up in Albert's bed, was a little, old, grey-haired lady. Tiny, frail, and very frightened.

"This is all your doing!" shouted Betty, grabbing Amos by his arm. "If you hadn't forced Albert to be a grown-up while she was still a child, none of this would ever have happened!"

Amos hung his head like a naughty child, kicked the floor with his shoe and said nothing.

TALES FROM THE SHOP THAT NEVER SHUTS
Martin Waddell

McGlone lives at the Shop that Never Shuts, and Flash and Buster Cook are in McGlone's Gang with wee Biddy O'Hare. In these five highly entertaining stories the Gang dig for Viking treasure, are frightened that a sea monster has eaten Biddy, discover that McGlone needs glasses, look after the Shop that Never Shuts on their own, and give Biddy a birthday party.

VERA PRATT AND THE BALD HEAD
Brough Girling

When Wally Pratt and his fanatic mechanic mother enter the Motorbike and Sidecar Grand Prix, nothing is really as it seems. Vera's old enemy, Captain Smoothy-Smythe, is up to his old tricks and suddenly Wally is kidnapped. Rescue him? She can't do that yet, she's got to win the Grand Prix first. Two minutes to go and Vera finds herself the ideal partner – a headmaster with no hair!

CRUMMY MUMMY AND ME
Anne Fine

How would you feel if your mother had royal-blue hair and wore lavender fishnet tights? It's not easy for Minna being the only sensible one in the family, even though she's used to her mum's weird clothes and eccentric behaviour. But then the whole family are a bit unusual, and their exploits make very entertaining and enjoyable reading.

BIG IGGY
Kaye Umansky

When large Lizzy decides it's time she had a bit of peace and quiet, Big Iggy – the smallest dragon – and his brothers all take off into the big wide world. But Big Iggy's first flight ends with a crash landing into a tree – and a huge adventure.

WITCHES IN STITCHES
Kaye Umansky

Your very own monster magazine! Jokes, interviews, competitions, quizzes, health and beauty, songs, poems, lonely hearts, horrorscopes, special offers – it's packed with original and totally unexpected fun.

BAGTHORPES LIBERATED
Helen Cresswell

In the seventh book about the eccentric Bagthorpe family, Mrs Bagthorpe is determined to liberate the female members of the household from domestic drudgery and sets out to rally support for her radical views. But a string of hilarious incidents proves all too clearly that if there is one thing Mrs Bagthorpe can never be, it's liberated.

SON OF A GUN
Janet and Allan Ahlberg

A galloping, riotous wild west farce in which the plot thickens with every page until a combined force of Indians, US cavalry, old-timers, dancing-girls and the 8-year-old hero are racing to the rescue of a mother and baby, besieged in their cabin by two incompetent bandits called Slocum. As one of the Slocums says, 'Cavalry *and* Indians? Where's the fairness in that?' – *The New Statesman*

HENRY AND RIBSY
Beverly Cleary

Henry's dream is to go fishing with his father. He can just see himself sitting in a boat, reeling in an enormous salmon, Mr Huggins has promised he will take Henry fishing on one condition: that he keeps Ribsy out of trouble and does not let him annoy the neighbours, especially Mr Grumble next door. The trouble is, keeping a dog like Ribsy under control isn't that easy!

WILL THE REAL GERTRUDE HOLLINGS PLEASE STAND UP?
Sheila Greenwald

Gertrude is in a bad way. She's a bit slow at school but everyone thinks she's dumb and her teachers call her 'Learning Disabled' behind her back. As if this isn't enough, her parents go off on a business trip leaving her with her aunt and uncle and her obnoxious cousin, Albert – a 'super-achiever'. Gertrude is determined to win Perfect Prize-Winning Albert's respect by whatever means it takes . . .

THE REVOLTING BRIDESMAID
Mary Hooper

When Katie's sister Gillian announces that she is marrying the appalling Christopher, Katie is horrified. When she realizes she is expected to be bridesmaid, she thinks she's going to be sick! Can she possibly find Gillian a more exciting alternative groom in two months?

PLAYING WITH FIRE
Anthony Masters

The new St Elmer's Primary School has been built on the site of an ancient abbey, and everyone is talking about the monks who used to live there. Will their ghosts be found sitting at spare desks at the back of the class?

Of course, no one really believes any of the silly rumours, but when term begins, the teachers begin to behave very oddly. Chris and Tim are determined to uncover the truth behind some of the peculiar goings-on.

HARVEY'S ARK
Robin Kingsland

You may think ace space pilot Harvey is bananas when he launches into space with his all-animal crew. But when a meteor knocks them off course and their spaceship lands on Phungos 5 – the Paradise Planet – it's Harvey who saves the day and it's Harvey who makes a dream come true for Ozalid Crust!

A zany space adventure for readers from every planet!

WOLF
Gillian Cross

Cassy has never understood the connection between the secret midnight visitor to her nan's flat and her sudden trips to stay with her mother. But this time it seems different. She finds her mother living in a squat with her boyfriend Lyall and his son Robert. Lyall has devised a theatrical event for children on wolves, and Cassy is soon deeply involved in presenting it. Perhaps too involved – for she begins to sense a very real and terrifying wolf stalking her.

THE OUTSIDE CHILD
Nina Bawden

Imagine suddenly discovering you have a step-brother and -sister no one has ever told you about! It's the most exciting thing that's ever happened to Jane, and she can't wait to meet them. Perhaps at last she will become part of a 'proper' family, instead of for ever being the outside child. So begins a long search for her brother and sister, but when she finally does track them down, Jane finds there are still more surprises in store!

THE FOX OF SKELLAND
Rachel Dixon

Samantha's never liked the old custom of Foxing Day – the fox costume especially gives her the creeps. So when Jason and Rib, children of the new publicans at The Fox and Lady, find the costume and Jason wears it to the fancy-dress disco, she's sure something awful will happen.

Then Sam's old friend Joseph sees the ghost of the Lady and her fox. Has she really come back to exact vengeance on the village? Or has her appearance got something to do with the spate of of burglaries in the area?